The Golden Door

Gregory M. Thompson

TO JAMISON

when you're older

Other Books by Gregory M. Thompson

Nightcry

Underneath the Trees (poetry)

ACKNOWLEDGMENTS

Would this book be possible without the help of others? First, thanks to my lovely wife and all the support she's given me so far to let me continue to write down a few words here and there. Also, thanks to my beta readers Teresa Kubalanza, Andrew Saxsma and Michelle Sussman: without any of your eyes, the world would see a few more mistakes than I had intended. Lastly, thanks to you, my readers. Your support on my first novel and your encouraging words fill me with inspiration…to tell you more scary stories.

With that said, the golden door awaits you…

CHAPTER ONE

June 20

Adam didn't want to go into his mother's bedroom, but she had asked for him. He knew death hovered like a balloon over his mother, its lips probably smacking with giddy delight. He placed his sweaty and shaking palm around the doorknob anyway and twisted, hoping the door, the room behind it and the impending doom would disappear around him. Fourteen was too young to be without a mother.

After lightly shoving the door inward, Adam took a step inside the bedroom. The avalanche of smells made him cringe and he covered his mouth with his right hand to keep his lunch down. Beer was the immediate and instantly recognizable smell. Adam noticed his father slumped in an old, brown La-Z-Boy recliner; a bottle of beer hung from his fingertips. Adam wondered when his father last took a shower. His father's oily hair glimmered in the light of dusk and dark smudges of dirt or grease or whatever it was pressed deep into the cracks of his aging face.

The vibrating snores of his father shook the arm holding the bottle and Adam expected the bottle to fall to its death at any moment. Like a dutiful son, Adam considered removing the bottle, then tossed the thought aside. *What if he wakes up and wants a beer really bad and remembers he had a bottle in his hand when he went to sleep and when he lifts his hand to take sip, it won't be there and then he'll be angry and will want you to get a tree branch for switchin' time. No: better just to leave it there.*

A deep, rotten meat scent was the second smell. Adam sniffed the air again and he recalled the time he didn't finish washing the dishes and they sat out for days. During that time, the food left behind quickly rotted and contaminated the air with a hollow, biting stench that tattled on Adam when his father came home the day his accident happened at the factory. Adam never forgot to wash the dishes again.

Much to the surprise of Adam, a third smell caressed his nose. Rose petals, Adam guessed. The scent hung in the air between the other two disgusting smells. Adam stepped in further and noticed an oval decanter of perfume sitting on the nightstand. *Silent Rose* was stamped on the sticker affixed to the front side. Adam and Tommy had pooled their money together last year and got the perfume for her birthday. The perfume cost them $12 and they just had enough and they knew it wasn't going to be like the stuff J-Lo or Britney Spears sold, but their mother always told them when you give gifts, don't worry about what you get because it's the thought that counts. And she wore it almost every day.

It's the thought that counts.

"Adam—" His mother's voice cracked. It didn't sound healthy. She let loose with a cough and turned her head towards Adam. "Adam. You are here." A slow, methodological spewing of words.

"I am, mother."

"Come here." She paused to catch her breath. "I want to talk to you."

Adam glanced at his father and walked across the bedroom when he thought it was safe. In case his father suddenly woke up and caught Adam in the bedroom, Adam had a quick plan of escape: dive under the bed. His father frowned upon Adam and his brother constantly visiting their mother during her sickness. *She'll never get better if you two shitbirds keep buggin' her*, he'd say.

Adam didn't acknowledge his mother until he stood next to the bed in order to focus all his power on being stealthy.

"How are you feeling?" Adam asked. It was a stupid question, he knew. The sickness had burrowed itself inside and lived in her for nine months. Nine months tomorrow, to be exact. Adam looked at the floor; how silly could he be for tallying the days?

"I'm dying Adam. This cancer has been eating me alive for a year." A cough. "I am ready to leave this place."

"No. You just need some rest."

"I'll be getting plenty of that soon."

A rough grunt came from the corner. Adam watched his father shift slightly in the chair, the bottle of beer still secure.

"Adam, come closer. I want to tell you something."
His mother tried to move so her whole body faced him,
but he stopped her.

"Mom, no. Just stay still." Adam leaned in. "What do
you want to say?"

"It's about your father."

"What about him?"

"I want you to be wary of him."

"Wary? What does that mean?"

"Keep an eye on him."

Adam nodded. "Of course. Tom and I will take care
of him."

"I didn't mean—"Another cough. "I didn't mean like
that. You and your brother need to watch out for him.
He's not a pleasant person."

"I don't understand."

A weak hand emerged from under the covers and
lightly touched Adam's cheek. Adam enjoyed the quick
contact from his mother, even though it took a good
amount of effort from her.

"Don't trust him," his mother said. "Ever."

His mother scooted up, but she struggled. She placed
her arms under her body to hoist what she could, but
Adam saw the trouble she was having. Adam got his
arms under her back and lifted and pulled her toward the
headboard.

When his mother was propped against the headboard
and regained some of her strength back, she said, "You're
strong. You should play sports when you become a
sophomore this school year."

"I've been thinking about it."

His mother reached over and slowly lowered the
shoulder part of her nightgown. This motion revealed a

three- or four-inch gash oozing blood. The edges of the cut had started to turn black and small flakes of older blood slipped onto his mother's fresher skin.

"Your father did that to me weeks ago," she said. "It has never healed properly." She returned the sleeve back to her shoulder. "Not that it matters now, anyway," his mother added.

"He would never hurt *us*," Adam said.

"I know he won't," she said.

With some of her last strength, his mother reached over with both hands and cupped Adam's face. "I'll make sure of that," she said.

"How?"

"Don't worry about that. You worry about your summer; you worry about getting ready for the next school year; you worry about girls; you worry about everything else besides how I'll make sure your father doesn't hurt you." His mother looked over to his father and then continued, "I'm making you a promise right now that he won't and that I will make his life a living hell."

Adam shook his head. "Buy why? I know he won't hurt us."

"You can't be sure, Adam."

"Neither can you, mom. You're too weak."

"Though the body is weak," his mother said, "the will is strong."

"I don't want you to promise that. I want you to promise you won't die."

Adam saw sympathy shoot from his mother's eyes. *Why is she giving* me *the sympathy?* At that moment he knew she couldn't promise that, but hoped the next words out of her mouth would be just that.

"I am human and the cancer is beyond my control." She slid back down into the bed; this was easier for her. Adam made an attempt to help her, but his mother shook her head. "You are a sweet boy, Adam. Soon, the girls will be begging you to make them happy."

"Mom…" Adam sensed tears welling, bulking up like a clogged drain that didn't want to be unclogged.

"Don't cry. Give me a hug."

Adam raised his arms and intertwined them with his mother's arms. They embraced for a minute as Adam soaked in every ounce of love his mother released. Adam realized this was the last hug he would receive from his mother and the tears flowed. His mother patted the back of Adam's head.

"I love you, Adam."

"I love you too, mom."

She gave him a final squeeze and Adam pulled away. "I have to rest now," she said.

Defeated, Adam stepped back. His mother relaxed her head, her eyes gazing toward the ceiling. Adam watched his mother's eyes roll up into her head.

This is it, Adam thought. *I'm going to watch her die.* He wished his father was awake and Tommy was standing here. Really, he only wanted Tommy next to him. Adam wondered why his mother had just called him and not Tommy too. Wasn't she also afraid of his father waking up or worse, pretending to be asleep and hearing everything they said? He would be angry and ready to do some *switching*. But his father didn't wake and Tommy wasn't here; he was forced to watch his mother die.

He was forced to do it alone.

A light gasp escaped his mother's mouth. Her lips vibrated for a split second and then her head lolled to the right, facing Adam. The eyes remained open, but no life remained. Adam took a step towards her to close the eyelids, but stopped: he didn't want to give his father any reason to think he'd been in the bedroom.

With no other reason to stay in the room, Adam turned and caught a glimpse of his father. For a second, Adam thought his father *had* awakened and watched him behind blurry and inebriated eyes. *Hey son, watch ya guys talkin' about over there? Havin' a little mother-son talk about stuff? Well, tell me this stuff, eh son? Your good old involved father wants to know this stuff. If you don't start tellin' me what you and your whore mother were talkin' about, I'm goin' to have you pick out a nice little branch for a wonderful switchin' time!*

This was not the case though: his father choked on a snore and continued sleeping.

Adam relaxed.

Sneaking across the floor to leave the room just as he had to reach his mother, Adam made it to the bedroom door without incident. His father stayed sleeping; the beer continued to hang perilously over the floor; and the Death Scent hit Adam even harder as he passed through the doorway into the hall. The Scent became stronger somehow since the passing of his mother.

Adam quietly shut the door and went into the bathroom. The lock to this door was broken and Adam pushed the clothes hamper in front of the door. After swiping the shower curtain back, Adam stepped into the tub and sat down. He just needed a few minutes.

The few minutes turned into thirty as he let fly all of the tears.

CHAPTER TWO

Two weeks later.

Adam flipped his 10-speed over so the seat and handlebars balanced the bike on the ground. As he spun the pedals, he saw the chain just a little off from the gears. On closer inspection, one of the gear's teeth was missing. Adam sighed. *Make it through one more summer, my friend. Just one more. I know you can do it.* He adjusted the chain to see if there was a way the gap could be avoided, but he had no luck. The chain continued to slip each time it passed over the space.

"Are you fixing that bike *again?*"

Tommy bounded down the porch stairs holding a baseball and a mitt. Tommy's thick, dark hair spilled out from under his Chicago Cubs baseball hat; the strands waved at Adam as Tommy moved across the yard. He wore his favorite T-shirt that said '*T-Ball is for babies; Baseball is for men.*' The jeans, ripped at the knees, were not the best, but if Tommy decided to play rough or get dirty, the jeans would suffice. It would soon be time to get new school clothes anyway, if his father took on any jobs between now and then.

"How many times can you fix it?" He asked.

Adam knew Tommy didn't ask because he really wanted to know how many times the bike could be fixed; Tommy asked to be difficult. Tommy was great at being difficult. Worse, Tommy knew when he was being difficult and sometimes relished it. What a hobby for a nine-year-old.

"It's not that big a deal," Adam said. "I've fixed this problem before."

"We'll see."

Tommy sat on the ground a few feet from Adam and set down his mitt and ball. Tommy fiddled with the rear tire when Adam reached down for a pair of pliers. Adam swiped his brother's hand away. Tommy pushed down on the baseball and rolled it into the dirt as if he were rolling a ball of clay.

Adam stopped fixing his bike. "What is it, Tommy?" he asked.

The answer was a shrug.

"If you have something to say," Adam said, "then say it. Don't dilly-dally around. I got a bike to fix."

"I miss mom," Tommy said.

"I know. So do I."

"I wish she was in the kitchen right now, making us lunch."

"Yeah. BLTs, right? That would be good."

Tommy laughed. "Or even bologna and cheese."

"That's boring. BLTs make the perfect summer lunch."

"Maybe she could make them both."

"She would, too," Adam said, nodding.

"I still miss her."

Adam picked up the baseball mitt. "Remember when mom took you to get this last year? You didn't want to play baseball. You said it was stupid. That hitting a ball with a stick didn't make sense. What eight-year-old says stuff like that?" A smile crossed Tommy's face. "You say stuff like that. But she bought you the mitt anyway and pretty much dragged you on the field when it was time for your first game."

"I remember."

"And what happened when you went for your first at-bat?"

"I hit the ball."

"Right! You hit the ball! And you hit it pretty good. Got to first base, didn't you?" Tommy nodded. "After that, you couldn't stop talking about baseball. When the season ended, you couldn't wait for this summer."

"I'm playing pretty good this year," Tommy said, beaming.

"You sure are. And mom knows you are too."

"What do you mean?"

"That mitt. She's with you every time you put that mitt on."

Tommy slipped the mitt on his hand, pushing the fingers in the slots securely. Something said, *Yes she is* in that movement. Tommy was proud to have the mitt on at that moment. *He may never take it off now,* Adam thought, which would be all right with him. Adam would understand.

With Tommy focused on the mitt, Adam snatched the baseball from the ground and tossed it into the air a couple of times.

"Go out for a throw," Adam commanded. "We have to keep you loose for next year's season."

Tommy leapt up and took off running across the yard. With a big house came a big yard and long fence to surround it. Before his mother passed, his mother, Tommy and him spent many cool spring evenings looking at the stars, guessing which constellations were which. Tommy usually took the guesses; Adam was usually right. He missed that. Maybe he could talk Tommy into camping in the back yard tonight or tomorrow night and they could play the Constellation Guessing game.

Adam rose and waited until his brother hit the thick oak tree—which sat about fifty feet away—and gave a hefty throw. The ball sailed upward and went to a perfect arc towards Tommy, who had just turned around when the ball was halfway to him.

"Nice throw!" Tommy yelled.

"Better make it a nice catch!" Adam responded.

And Tommy did make it a nice catch. The ball hit the glove with a *thwaaaappp* and Tommy closed the mitt around it. He raised the glove into the air as if to say, *I made this phenomenal catch everyone, now where's that scout from the Yankees to sign me to a five-year deal?*

Tommy sprinted back to Adam.

Adam gave Tommy a light punch on his arm. "Good catch. I'd say you're ready for next year."

The brothers sat back down on the ground in front of Adam's bike. Adam picked up the pliers again and went to work removing the nut from the rear wheel axle.

"Do you think dad misses mom?" Tommy asked.

The nut loosened and Adam removed it the rest of the way with his fingers before answering the question.

"I'm sure he does." Adam guided the wheel from its slot on the frame and laid it on the ground. "Dad was with her until the very end," Adam said. It wasn't really a lie; Adam just wasn't going to tell Tommy that Dad was sleeping off his recent drunk spell and probably happened to land in the chair in the bedroom. A nine-year-old shouldn't hear that about his father. Tommy already knew that their father drank daily and disappeared constantly anyway, even more since their mother passed away, so tainting their mother's death didn't appeal to Adam.

"Yeah, he probably misses her then," Tommy said. The agreement didn't sound too believable to Adam, but he let it go. This bike needed more attention at the moment than Tommy's concern for their father's grief, if it existed at all.

Tommy stood. "I'm going next door to see if Jill wants to play catch," he said.

"Okay. Say hi to your girlfriend for me."

"I will—wait!" They laughed for a moment. "She's not my girlfriend," Tommy said.

"If you say so."

As Tommy reached the gate, Adam heard the rear porch door to the house open. Adam focused on taking the chain off since he knew his father had been drinking most of the day and particularly didn't want to catch his eyes.

"Where the hell is that shitbird going?" Joe muttered.

Adam continued to look at his bike. "He said he was going next door to play catch with Jill." When Adam heard *shitbird,* he knew his dad was in a bad, drunk place. For the past month or so, he heard *shitbird* almost every day so hearing it now didn't really faze Adam; he just knew how to handle his father the rest of the day.

And that meant very, *very* carefully.

"Make sure he's back before dinner or both of you wily little shitbirds are gonna get a damn good switchin'. I'll be gone for a bit."

"Are *you* going to be back by dinner?" The question hovered in the air for a moment and Adam wished he could reach out, grab the question and stuff it back into his brain. To that tiny spot in his head marked for *Stupid Questions That Will Get You Switched*.

It only took his father three heavy steps with his steel-toed work boots to reach Adam. "*What* did you ask me?" He demanded. "If you asked me what I think you asked me, you might want to think of another question that won't have such bad consequences."

"Did someone hire you to do something?" Adam asked instead.

"Why would you ask that?"

Adam pointed to his father's boots. He wore them every day for the past seven years at the factory. After he was fired or he quit or was laid off—which was what his father sometimes told people—he only wore the slowly-deteriorating boots when someone hired him to do some handy work like mow the grass, fix shutters or clean out pools: basically *shitbird* work.

His father looked down. "I can't wear the boots without you asking about them?" He walked around Adam and gazed down at the bike. "Havin' a little trouble with the bike there, son? Let me see if I can help you."

Pretending to reach down and grab a tool, Adam's father gripped the top tube with both of his hands. He looked awkward doing it since the bike was upside down.

Adam saw one of the boot's tongue flap out, mocking Adam: *Hey buddy, I just decided to come out and see what kind of switchin' you're goin' to get. Oh yes, you're going to get one, believe me on that. Mr. Cranky up there is probably going to drink some more—because we both know he's not goin' to a job—and come home and find one little reason to give you a switchin'. Better pick out a light stick this time; you don't want it to hurt that bad.*

With one motion, Joe lifted the bike into the air and hurtled it about twenty feet across the yard. The bike rolled another few feet, the chain clanking against the frame. Two spokes snapped from the rim and flew to the side. The wheel made one complete turn and stopped, not because it was time for the wheel to stop, but because a bent portion of the rim jutted into the two brake pads.

"Dad!" Adam ran to the bike, checking out the damage. Any repairs the biked needed were beyond what Adam could do.

"Did that fix it?" His father asked, followed by a small chuckle.

Adam felt his body tingle; the frustration of his father's action caused a tear to make its way out. He held back a blubber by biting his lower lip.

His father shook his head. "You gonna cry now? It's just a damn bike. You're lucky that wasn't you flying through the air you ungrateful shitbird." He headed towards the gate.

"*MOM WOULD NEVER LET YOU ACT LIKE THIS!*" Adam screamed. It just came out before he could suppress it. His father's reaction wouldn't be good, but Adam felt relieved to have screamed it.

Adam saw his father hesitate before going completely through the gate. To Adam's surprise, his father pushed the gate open and disappeared through it. He didn't know if that was worse or if he would rather have had his father get angry on the spot and deal out any punishment immediately.

Did that fix it?

Adam sat on the ground and put his head in his hands. He wanted things different, of course, but what could a fourteen-year-old kid with a nine-year-old brother do? The only parent they had spent most of the time drunk and yelling at them and any neighbors who they thought might care didn't, because if they did, they'd have interfered long ago.

Maybe he'd ask Victor his thoughts. He hadn't seen Victor since the funeral. Even when things died down, he and Victor hadn't hung out.

Tomorrow, Victor.

Adam looked at his watch, reminding himself to get Tommy in for dinner in an hour, just to be safe. Then, he gathered any loose pieces that managed to spring free of the bike and returned to his fix-it spot and started the process of reassembling the bike as best he could.

CHAPTER THREE

Two hours, Twenty Minutes Later

Dinner consisted of frozen TV dinners, as it did most nights. Adam prepared a Salisbury steak for himself, a Macaroni and Meat for Tommy and a three-piece fried chicken Hungry Man meal for his father. The brothers waited patiently at the table, which they did every night because their father never made it on time for dinner. Sometimes it was a few minutes later and sometimes it was hours later. Adam and Tommy still sat at the table, no matter what time he got home. Twice, Adam made Tommy sit at the table by himself to keep a lookout for their father so Adam could finish some Algebra homework. Adam was sure his father didn't know about either times and neither brother wanted to push their luck and try for additional deceptions.

"I'm hungry," Tommy said.

"It's only been twenty minutes," Adam responded. "You can hold on a little longer."

Tommy picked up his fork and pushed it into his macaroni. He slid it around the black, plastic tray like a mop. "Just one bite?" He finally asked.

"Hey, if you want to be the one that pisses dad off tonight, go ahead."

Adam watched the forked return to its place on the table. He smiled. "That's what I thought."

The kitchen door swung open, bouncing from the wall and into Joe as he came through. He carried two gallon-sized cans of paint and set them on the floor. Adam and Tommy watched him with apprehension. Their father stepped back outside and returned with two more cans of paint and stacked them on top of the others. The third time, Joe set two plastics sacks on the kitchen counter. Adam peered at the bags and thought he saw paint brushes and stirrers inside.

His father glanced from Adam to Tommy and then to their dinners in front of them. "Where's mine?" He asked.

Adam pointed to the microwave.

Joe opened the microwave and removed his dinner. Detouring to the fridge, he grabbed a beer, and then plopped down at the table. In one swift motion, Joe scooped up a huge blob of mashed potatoes and shoved them in his mouth. Seconds later, the mashed potatoes came spilling out, back into the tray.

"Which one of you shitbirds cooked this?" He asked, calmly. The last couple of words shot out with hoarseness.

"I did," Adam answered.

"It's cold."

"You're almost thirty minutes late." Adam put a bit of his own food in his mouth, chewed, then said, "I thought you said you'd be back at six."

"I don't have to be." Joe slid the tray to Adam. "Reheat this and then go outside and find yourself a branch. You're getting a switchin' because my food is cold and you are talking back."

Adam rose, but his body slumped, making him look like he was almost bending over uncomfortably. He snatched the tray and stuck it back into the microwave and set it for two minutes. While he stood there, he peeked out of the kitchen window. He'd have to cut a branch from the oak tree since the other two trees were dying. The dry, brittle branches would not do what his father wanted, which was to create whip marks on his skin. The dead branches would just snap off, probably angering his dad more.

In those two minutes, Adam contemplated the branch he planned on cutting. He saw it about nine feet up with very few leaves on it. That meant the branch was alive just enough to satisfy his father, but dead enough to cause little pain. He'd have to get the ladder from the garage; at least he could choose his own branch, which Adam considered a positive. The branch wouldn't mark him too bad, depending on how many switches his father wanted to lay on him and Adam hoped the punishment was light for cold food and talking back.

"What's the paint for?" Tommy asked.

Don't, Adam thought. *Don't provoke him.*

"It's for painting, dumbass."

"Painting what?"

"The wall in the mind your own business."

Tommy knew when to stop talking, and this moment was it. Adam quickly turned grateful.

The microwave dinged and Adam took out the tray using a kitchen towel. Without a word, he set the steaming food in front of his father.

"You know what to do now," Joe said.

Adam nodded morosely. When he took a step towards the door, he heard his father tap the table impatiently.

"Don't forget your dinner." Joe said. "Eat it out there; I'll be out in a bit."

Grabbing the tray and a fork, Adam hurried to leave the kitchen. When he opened the door, his father yelled, "Make sure you make it a big switchin' stick!" A huge, hearty laugh followed, which Adam heard all the way out to the oak tree.

Adam sauntered to the shed. When he reached the door, he noticed at some point, his father had unlocked the door. Probably in the time he left for wherever he was going and when he walked through the door with the paint.

The shed contained all of his father's tools collected over the past thirty years or so. Most of the tools were from the era in his twenties when he worked as a mechanic's apprentice—very few of the tools were recent. His father loved Craftsman tools and despite that—especially since they had lifetime guarantees—rust, stains and chips existed on almost every single tool in the shed. Some of the tools remained in better condition, but his father never went to Sears to exchange them for something better, something newer. On many occasions, Adam had even offered to take the tools in for him but his father always said the same thing, *I grew up with these exact tools; they gave me the money I once had and they remind me of the money I'll have once again.*

Adam stopped asking to take the tools a year ago.

The money you'll have again is never going to come, Adam thought.

Adam glanced over the tools. *At least the shed is organized.* Most of the smaller tools lived in three large, multi-drawer tool boxes. The middle toolbox's top lid gaped open, ready to swallow him if necessary.

Need a tool, young man? The toolbox mocked. *The tool you need isn't in here, but I'll be glad to let you reach in and grab something. I won't bite, I promise. Why would I risk being switched and thrown away? Your father takes better care of the tools I hold than you and Tommy.*

"Shut up," Adam murmured.

The tool you need is right above me, it said. *Go ahead, get it.*

The long, thin saw with the curved, wooden handle made for one hand was above the middle toolbox and was the best saw to cut branches. Adam thought about using one of the other saws—which included a hacksaw, a bow saw and a larger wood saw—but he didn't want to risk dulling the blade or bending the teeth on any of them. His father allowed one and only one saw to cut Switching Branches.

Adam pushed the two-step stool in front of the middle toolbox and climbed up. Before reaching for the saw, he unhooked the hinge on the toolbox and shut the lid.

Awww, come on Adam, how am I going to bite you now?

"You're not."

That's too bad. My bite isn't as worse as Joe's switchin'.

Adam grabbed the saw and quickly stepped back onto the floor. He replaced the stool—nothing out of place now—and stood in the doorway of the shed.

Inside the kitchen, Adam saw his father and Tommy eating their dinner. No talking, just chewing. For a moment, Adam was glad he was out here and not at the table, uncomfortably eating his dinner as his father sat there staring .

He felt bad for Tommy, though. At least both of them weren't getting in trouble tonight.

Adam went around the side of the shed and lowered the aluminum ladder that hung horizontally on the wall. He would have to drag the heavy ladder to the tree and the bottom feet would leave ruts in the yard, but Adam couldn't think of any other way to get the one branch he wanted. No other branch would do at this point.

He tried to hoist the ladder over his head and carry the thing like a true construction worker, but the length caused Adam to become unbalanced and he couldn't compensate very well for the change in weight. *I'm a fulcrum*, Adam thought. As one end of the ladder kissed the ground, he chuckled.

It would have to be the dragging technique. At least if he father got angry about the ruts, he could just add onto to the switchin' since his father was going to do it anyway. Five, ten, fifteen: after a while, it got easier to forget about the numbers.

Working backwards, Adam pulled the ladder to the oak tree and opened the sides into an 'A' next to the branch. The top of the ladder went another foot over the branch, which pleased Adam; he wouldn't have to stand on the top rung and worry about falling. Adam tucked the saw in the waistband of his pants and carefully climbed the ladder.

Eight steps later, he figured he was high enough. He shook the ladder with his weight just to make sure the base was secure enough to hold him and the movement of his cutting.

"That looks like a good one!" He heard his father say.

Adam glanced behind him and saw his father holding the frozen dinner tray, eating and watching Adam as he prepared to cut the branch.

"Hey Tommy," his father said. "Come here and watch your brother."

"I don't want to," Tommy said.

"Do you want to get your own switch?"

Tommy reluctantly made his way into the doorway, standing next to their father. Even though he stood there, Tommy tried *not* to look.

"Dad, he doesn't *want* to," Adam forced.

"Cut the damn thing!" His father threw his dinner on the ground. "So we can get moving and you can cook me another dinner!"

Adam knew if he didn't cut the branch soon, both he and Tommy would pay for their father's anger.

He turned back to the branch and started cutting a three-foot piece of the branch. If it was too short, his father wouldn't like it; if the branch was too long, his father wouldn't like it; the branch had to be just right. The branch was the porridge from the *Goldilocks* story and his father was Goldilocks.

Adam smiled and chuckled again. He imagined his father in a blue and white dress with long, yellow hair sampling different branches.

This branch is way too short, he imagined his father saying. *See how the branch gets no leverage for a good whip? That's not going to leave any mark on you, Adam. This branch is way, way too long. It's too awkward to handle and I can't hit the spot I want. I need to hit the super-soft fleshy part of your thighs and all I can hit with this long branch is your back or other parts of your leg.*

His father picked up the perfect branch in Adam's mind. *Ah, yes, Adam. This one here is perfect. Good weight, good length. I can control this one and give you the best marks you've ever seen. Son, you've picked the best branch of your life; now get ready for the best switchin' of your life.*

Adam paused cutting.

Was this the right branch? Could he pick a less menacing one? He glanced around the oak tree and found a couple more that might do the job, but didn't think there was time to move the ladder and start a fresh process. This one would have to do.

Should have thought this through more.

The branch fell from the tree with three more sawing motions and landed on the ground below. From near the top of the ladder, the branch looked less intimidating and Adam thought the branch would serve its purpose honorably.

Adam climbed back down, dragged the ladder back to the shed and returned it to the side wall. On the way back to the branch, Adam attempted to cover in the ruts by pressing his foot over the top of the soil, hoping some of the grass and dirt would fill it back in. Some of the rut closed up, but it was still very noticeable.

"Dad!" Adam called out.

His father emerged in the doorway again. "It's about time," was all his father said.

Adam held the branch out as his father approached. His father took the branch and circled his hand around it and poked the branch through and back again, like he was skinning it. "How did you find one so smooth?" He asked.

"I don't know."

"Well, pants down, lie on your stomach."

As Adam did as told, he watched his father smack the branch into his hand a couple of times. "Fine branch you cut."

With his pants around his ankles, Adam knelt down and eased onto the ground, lying on his stomach.

"Boxers up," his father said.

Almost forgot, Adam thought. He reached back and pulled up his boxer's legs so the rear of his thighs became exposed. He felt a light breeze wash over the tiny hairs and Adam shivered, then lowered his head into the grass. He hoped the grass would muffle his screams.

The first crack came without warning. More of a caressing touch, really, which Adam thought meant to prepare for better aim. The hit still stung and Adam winced into the ground.

"That's better," he heard his father whisper.

The next five whacks slammed into his thighs like machine gun fire. Each thread of pain rocked his body, forcing him to scream into the grass. The back of his thighs seared with heat and Adam felt tiny trickles of blood rolling down his skin. When there was a pause in the switching, Adam turned his head to the side, his eyes watering from the throbbing pain. There was something in his father's strikes that was more animal than usual; more determined than previous switchings. It was like his father *wanted* to make him bleed.

"Let me get you a bottle, you little infant," his father said. He tossed the branch next to Adam's head.

The top quarter of the branch had bent and he saw the sinewy, green insides of the stick. A fresh branch, still alive. The end of the stick had streaks of blood staining the wood. At least it was over.

His father's feet ambled away towards the house. When his dad disappeared into the house, Adam rolled on his back. That was a mistake: the blades of grass poked the fresh gashes on his thighs, stinging sharply. Adam quickly tilted to his side and pulled up his jeans. He laid there for a minute longer, catching his breath and some of his pride.

When the pain on his thighs dulled, Adam rose. The muscles in that area quivered as he took a step and for a moment, he thought his rubber legs would give up on him. They didn't. Adam slowly made his way to the house.

Aspirin. He needed aspirin. Hopefully, his father was not in the kitchen and Adam could get the bottle of aspirin and take it to his room. As he stepped through the back kitchen door, Adam only saw his brother.

Tommy turned from his dinner and gave Adam a forced smile.

"Does it hurt?" He asked.

"A little."

"Thighs?"

Adam nodded. "Gonna get some aspirin and stay in my room."

"You should eat."

"I ate enough."

"Okay."

Adam knew Tommy was just trying to help. He just wanted to go to his room, lie down and start a new day. A new day to fix his bike; a new day to hang out with Victor; a new day without the threat of being switched.

"Where's dad?" Adam asked.

"I don't know. I think he went upstairs."

Adam looked down and saw the paint and sacks weren't there anymore. He opened the pill bottle, removed two capsules and sucked down water directly from the faucet. He swiped his mouth with his sleeve and thought a moment about grabbing something to eat. A snack at this point. But really, he didn't feel hungry.

"Want to play a game or something?" Tommy asked.

"No. Just want to be alone in my room."

"Maybe later?"

"Fine," Adam said, relenting.

"Great! What game?"

Adam was already halfway out of the kitchen. He turned and said, "Surprise me. Just give me a couple hours."

In his room, Adam laid down on his bed. He expected Tommy to interrupt Adam's late nap in thirty minutes or so. *Two hours is a lifetime for a little brother.* Adam knew, he used to be nine.

Even though his bedroom door was completely shut, Adam heard scuffling and scraping noises coming from down the hall. They resonated through the wall, filtering into his room with a ghostly arrival. When one set of noises disappeared, a new set of strange noises took their place. Adam listened for a few moments and quickly became indifferent to the sounds since his thighs took up most of his brain's attention.

He fell asleep to these noises.

CHAPTER FOUR

The Next Afternoon

Adam tossed a palm-sized rock through a window of an abandoned warehouse. One section of the window—which was separated into ninths—crashed inward, creating a hole that let Adam and his friend Victor only see darkness. They had been throwing rocks for hours, shifting spots when windows in their throwing range ran out of glass. The railroad tracks provided the rocks, which were perfect in weight and perfect for throwing. When they started the day, they placed the rocks on the train tracks themselves because someone told Adam that trains get derailed since the rocks dislodge the metal wheels. Three trains came by within thirty minutes and not one of them derailed: the first two crushed the rock into powder while the third train shot the rock out like a slingshot. So they moved onto throwing rocks at the warehouse. Adam wished he could throw from inside the chain-link fence, but when they first arrived, they couldn't find any breach in the links.

Someone's care of the property boundary remained steadfast.

But now, hours later, Adam stopped grabbing rocks and ran his hand along the fence. He watched Victor throw rocks for a few minutes, one out of five actually hitting a window, before he mentioned his boredom.

"Yeah," Victor said. "I kinda wish we were in school."

Let's not go that far, Adam thought.

Victor bent over and selected another rock. Adam was a little jealous his friend's muscles becoming more defined recently and his height a few inches taller. Maybe that kind of stuff ran in Victor's family. *If my father is any indication of how I'll turn out, then I'm going to be a gawky weakling.*

Victor let the rock fly. One out of six now. His success continued to drop.

"Want to climb the fence? Go inside?"

Adam shook his head and pointed to the top of the fence. "Barbed wire. I don't want to get cut."

Most friends would ridicule a statement like that, comparing him to their grandma or their little sister, but Victor didn't act like that. Besides, he didn't have a little sister. Actually, Adam couldn't remember a time when Victor spoke or acted like a jerk to him. Victor was probably bored himself, Adam realized.

"What's with you?" Victor asked.

"What do you mean?"

"I haven't talk to you in days and we haven't hung out since last week. You okay?"

"Yeah. Just tired and bored."

"You sleeping?"

"Sure."

"Through the entire night?"

Victor knew all the answers to all his questions. Adam realized this, but his friend wanted to hear the answers anyway.

"Most of the night."

Victor tossed the rock he had in his hand to the ground. "Is it Joe?"

His friend knew much of what went on between his father and the rest of the world and because Victor held complete disdain for him, Victor called Adam's father by his first name. His father hated everyone, blamed everyone for the accident and talked down to anyone who said anything to him. Adam was sure Victor's father probably told him things about 'Joe the drunk' because 'Joe the drunk' was a well known moniker for him. Adam never outright mentioned the drunkenness or the whippings, though, but Victor was smart and Adam knew he could figure it out. Probably *had* figured it out.

"I know it is," Victor said, answering his own question. "You can't let him rule your life like that. It's one thing he's your father and fathers do rule our lives to a certain extent, but he's ruining yours. I consider my father a mentor and a disciplinarian. By rights, he can rule my life in that aspect." Victor took in a breath. "Your dad is just a plain old bastard. Drunk, inconsiderate, useless: I know he's your father, but he's not really a *father* now, is he?"

Adam found himself already shaking his head when the last part of the question came out. "I'm here, aren't I?" was all Adam could say.

"Is that all you want? To just be 'here'? You want to fix the situation, don't you?"

Adam nodded and said, "How did you get so smart?"

Victor laughed. "I like to read. And when you read, you learn shit." He looked ahead to the main road leading into the warehouse. "Let's see if we can push the gate open far enough to get in."

They raced to the entrance, Victor beating Adam by twenty feet. Besides muscle, Victor had speed. Adam grabbed the chain-link fence and took a few moments to catch his breath. "You're fast, Victor."

"Got me some strong legs, that's all."

It took them ten minutes, but they finally bent the gate open far enough for each of them to slip through. First Victor passed through the curled chain-link and held it back further so Adam could crawl through. Adam had to admit to himself that Victor did most of the work with his new summer strength, but luckily, his friend wouldn't rub that in.

Standing, they scoped out the building, trying to find a way in. Most of the windows rose higher than they could climb safely and on this side, Adam and Victor couldn't see a door. Victor pointed to the right half of the wall. "How about there?" He said.

Adam didn't see it right away, but realized Victor was talking about a ventilation grate. The metal slates looked loose and ready to fall with a slight tug; probably the perfect way inside.

"Sure," Adam answered.

On the way over, Victor said, "You've got to do something about it."

"About what?"

"You know. Your dad."

"Do what, exactly?" Adam scowled at Victor, who saw through it immediately.

"No, I didn't mean anything like hurting him or…" Victor shook his head. "Worse, killing him."

"Then what did you mean?"

"You've got to find help. Find help for your dad. Maybe get out of there."

"My dad would never get help."

"Have any relatives close by?"

Adam shook his head.

"You should at least tell someone. Maybe get some help on how to deal with Joe," Victor said.

"I've tried."

"Not hard enough."

They reached the grating and Victor yanked one of the slats away. "Yeah, this is the way in." He started on another slat, and then paused. "You going to think about flowers all day or you going to help me?"

Adam joined his friend and within minutes had the grate free of any obstructions.

"Give me a boost," Victor said.

Clasping his hands together, Adam intertwined his fingers and lifted when Victor placed a foot on the improvised lift. He watched Victor throw his upper half into the duct and quickly scurry inside. A second later, Victor's head popped out, followed by both of his hands.

"Grab on."

Adam did and his friend easily pulled him into the dark, metal duct.

Luckily, the other end was only fifteen feet ahead and didn't contain any slats. Small slivers of light lined the left part of the tiny tunnel, giving them just enough light to scoot towards the exit. Victor slid out and hit the floor with a concerning thud.

"I'm okay, Adam." A pause. "Be careful. It's about a six-foot drop."

To Adam, the drop felt like twenty feet as he glided out of the duct and floated to the cement floor. When he hit, Adam instinctively buckled his legs and rolled to a stop. Some pain shot through this hip, but he was fine. He stood.

"What do you think was here?" He asked Victor.

"No one remembers."

This part of the warehouse extended far. If Adam had to guess, he figured it spanned one block long and maybe half a block wide. Cement pillars were lined up and down the room, to hold up the structure as well as provide convenient blocks of space. Many of the pillars near the center of the room had short, plywood walls in between. To Adam's left rose a staircase that ended in a stilted room with windows that overlooked everything. *Probably the boss' tower*, Adam thought. Along the right hand wall were doors with various signs on them: he saw a men's and women's restroom, a door leading to a lounge, a conference room door and a cafeteria door.

"Look," Adam said, pointing, "they had a cafeteria."

This made Victor laugh. "Must have been a serious place."

They started walking across the dirt and leaf-ladened floor. The first pillar they reached had a clipboard nailed to the plaster. Victor grabbed it and started reading. "Production quotas for March. Employee output for February. Sounds like a little bit of the boring to me."

"Sounds like it." Adam glanced at the paper and saw columns of numbers that meant nothing to him. "But what did they *produce*? Where's the machinery?"

"They cleared it out years ago. You know that."

Adam did know that, but still wanted to know what this warehouse was used for. He could ask his dad, but he wouldn't know. His dad worked at the other warehouse in town before he hurt his foot. At least that warehouse was still operating and everyone knew what they made: shoes. Adam chuckled. *My dad hurt his foot at a shoe factory.*

"Maybe they made dildos," Victor said.

For a second, Adam sent the comment through this brain, trying to register what Victor said. *Did he really say that?* And when Adam was sure that Victor said, *Maybe they made dildos*, he burst out in laughter, propping himself against one of the pillars. This set Victor off and they laughed for what Adam was sure was five minutes. When they were done, Adam's stomach hurt, like it did when he had done too many sit-ups in gym class.

"That was a good one," Adam said.

"Got the idea from my mom." Victor made a circle with right hand's thumb and forefinger shoved his other forefinger in and out of the circle. "Maybe she got hers here."

Adam laughed again, but not as hard. Victor stopped his finger motion and looked out one of the windows. "Looks like it's getting dark outside," he said.

"It's supposed to storm this afternoon."

"We should go." Victor started towards the main doors. "We'll come back another time."

"Okay." Adam followed Victor to the door. For some reason, Adam wondered if their friendship would continue after this summer. And if it did, would it continue through the following year, through high school and college? If they didn't move away—*no one really moves away from here,* Adam thought—would they remain friends? Maybe when they're older, instead of exploring abandoned warehouses, they'd go fishing or sit in one of their garages drinking beer and complaining about women. But they'd still be friends. Adam feared that between the both of them, Victor would move away. Victor would probably go to a fancy college—not one of those community colleges no one's ever heard of. Victor would graduate and get a good-paying job, find a gorgeous wife and live life with new friends and hobbies. Adam knew that Victor didn't really need Adam's friendship; it was really the other way around and if Victor realized this or not, he never mentioned it. Regardless, Adam was grateful for Victor today.

The doors opened easily, which surprised Adam. They exited and Victor placed a large rock in the doorway to keep the door from shutting all the way.

"I don't want to climb through that thing again," he said.

"Agreed."

Once outside, Adam saw dark, low-lying clouds rolling by, creating a gray haze. While it hadn't started to rain yet, the storm was coming. Thunder erupted in the distance, rising to a crescendo before finally telling Adam it was time for it to go. The temperature had dropped at least ten degrees in the time they entered the warehouse to now.

"It's cold," Adam said. "Good storm weather."

"If you say so, Tom Skilling. I don't want to be caught in it."

Victor popped into a trot and Adam followed.

Adam left Victor at his house five minutes later, giving his friend a quick wave and arrived at his own house a couple minutes later. As he bounded up the stairs, the rain suddenly fell from the sky, as if to say, *Hey Adam: almost got you! Maybe next time. Maybe I'll get you the next time you're cutting down a branch for a good old time. Get you all drenched because wet skin hurts even more.*

He swung the front door open and jumped inside.

CHAPTER FIVE

That evening

Something was on their father's mind at dinner, Adam knew. He had watched his father *mull* over his dinner, not eating the entire frozen dinner of peas, mashed potatoes and stringy chicken. There were also no threats of *switchin'* or cursing or sarcastic comments and put-downs at dinner. At first, Adam thought he had done everything perfectly, but he had never known that to happen to anyone involved in his father's life. Adam considered asking what was wrong and quickly changed his mind: quiet is as quiet does. No sense in creating a problem.

After forty-five minutes, his dad shoved himself away from the table and finally said something. It was more of a mumble, though, and Adam still wasn't sure what his father said. Adam played the words out in his head and couldn't form any inclination what his father even meant.

Adam and Tommy watched him trudge into the hallway and stomp up the stairs. They didn't even say one word to each other; they didn't want to know what the problem was as long as it didn't include them. They cleared the table, had a few quick bites of ice cream and washed the few dishes they had used.

Now, Adam sat at the bottom of the stairs, his mind jumping from his book to figuring out what was wrong with his father. He was on Chapter 38 of *Moby Dick*, and couldn't really remember what the previous chapter had been about. Adam's eyes followed the words on the page, but interpreted no meaning. Chapter 38 was entitled "Dusk" and he knew the Chapter called "Moby Dick" was approaching. Though at this moment, the long exposition could not keep him motivated to continue reading.

As he shut the book, Tommy sprinted around the corner from the kitchen holding his glove and baseball.

"Whoa, Tommy. What's the hurry?"

"Nothing. Just playing some ball."

"Of course you are."

Tommy pointed to the book. "What are you reading?"

"*Moby Dick.*"

"Again? Why are you reading that before school has even started?"

"Because it's required reading this year and it's over 800 pages and I don't want to leave it for the last minute."

"But you already read it like a hundred times."

"Twice, actually. The last time was a year and a half ago."

Tommy flipped the baseball to Adam, whose slow reaction caused it to thump against the bottom step and roll back to Tommy.

"It's seven," Tommy said. "Go to the park with me and play catch."

"It rained earlier. It's probably all muddy and gross."

"Come *ooooon…*" Tommy snatched the ball and slipped on his glove. He slammed the ball into the glove over and over. "Just for a little bit. I got that rabid fever."

"The what?"

"Rabid fever. You know. When you're inside all the time."

"*Cabin* fever, Tommy, not rabid fever."

"Oh." Tommy stopped throwing the ball. "Just for thirty minutes. I promise."

Adam thought for a moment. The park was five minutes away, ten minutes round trip. That left twenty minutes to play catch. "Fine," Adam said, "thirty minutes from when we leave the house."

"Great!" Tommy ran to the front door and grabbed Adam's shoes. "Here!" He tossed them to Adam and they smacked him in the chest.

"Calm down, Tommy." Adam slipped on his tennis shoes. He looked up when he tied them to see Tommy all ready to go. *If he was that fast at doing his chores, we'd be all right with dad every night.*

"Catch!" Tommy yelled, but the ball was already in mid-air.

Adam noticed this wasn't a nice little toss, meant to travel a few feet to the intended target, Adam. This was a hurl. An all-out throw as if Tommy readied himself on an actual pitching mound waiting for the signal—

which he must have thought Adam had given *and* that signal had been a fastball request— and wound up his right arm and released the ball with all the force the fast ball needed to hit Tommy's top speed.

The ball sailed over Adam's head—he didn't need to duck at all—and continued an upwards trajectory over the stairs. It hit the top of the landing, finally coming down on the wooden floor with a low *grummmp!* Then, the ball rolled along the floor, bumping the wall and continuing to roll for another few seconds.

Adam looked at Tommy and whispered, "Nice going, Tommy Einstein. This isn't Wrigley Field."

Tommy shrugged and started walking up the stairs.

"What do you think you're doing?" Adam asked.

"Getting the ball."

Tommy continued to the top of the stairs and stopped, staring to the left. When his brother didn't move for another minute, Adam called up as quiet as he could but with enough volume, "Tommy, what's wrong?"

Finally, Tommy turned and waved for Adam to come up. Adam shook his head and Tommy waved again with more intensity.

"I hear something," Tommy whispered.

Adam crept up the stairs until he stood next to his brother. They stood there, breathing slowly and angling their ears to the sounds.

First, a scraping sound. Adam thought it sounded like sandpaper rubbing something. The monotonous sandpaper sound became louder at random moments and sometimes slowed until it was barely audible. Then, between the scraping, came a popping, rubbing sound. In the midst of all that, small, annoyed grunts. *Muh, muh.*

Then some mumbles. Indistinguishable, but definitely their father's. *Muh, muh, muh.*

Then a pause and the sounds started again with the scraping. Scrape, scrape, scrape. Pop, pop, pop; rub, rub, rub. *Muh, muh, muh.*

"What is that?" Tommy whispered.

"Shh!" Adam forced.

The sounds stopped for a moment and Adam put his hand on Tommy's shoulder, a silent command to not move one muscle. *It has to be our father,* Adam thought. And if he knew they were standing here, there would be days of incessant *switchin'*, each day rolling into one it would be so bad. Adam brought his finger to his lips and shook his head. *Just be quiet, Tommy. Just for a few moments.* Adam then pointed to each of them and then the stairs.

The sounds resumed, which relieved Adam.

Tommy shook his head. He mouthed, *I'm scared.*

Fine, Adam mouthed back.

With four strides, Adam hung by the corner leading to the adjacent hallway. Tommy reluctantly followed and planted his back against the wall. Adam leaned over and poked his head around the corner.

It was their father. He stood in the middle of a large mess of paint cans, brushes and paint trays. A two-step stool sat unopened against the left wall and some rags caked with dry and wet paint hung from the top. *At least he's using a drop-cloth*, Adam thought. *Maybe I won't get in trouble for the mess.* But Adam couldn't see a mess, really; everything looked pristine and drip-free. It actually surprised him that his father kept the area around whatever he was doing clean.

Whatever he was doing. What was he doing?

Muh, muh, muh. Grunts mixed with motions of painting and scraping. Adam now saw that it wasn't sandpaper, but a small metal scraper meant for removing chips of paint and other debris. The popping and rubbing sound was a paint roller going through the motions on the door. Up, down, up, down, a slight angle. Missed a spot, go back over.

His father was painting the door to his mother's bedroom.

And he was painting it gold.

Adam shifted back to Tommy. "Dad's painting," Adam said. He pointed around the wall's corner, and then gave Tommy a little shove to peek for himself.

Tommy eased along the wall, giving Adam a longing look of despair.

"It's okay," Adam whispered. "Look."

Tommy's head moved past the threshold and for one insane second, Adam thought it would be funny to push his little brother into the open hallway where their father could see him. Adam would then run downstairs and after their dad yelled at Tommy for a while—and told him exactly what kind of stick to get for his punishment—their no-humored father would look for Adam and he would pretend he wasn't upstairs at all saying he didn't know what Tommy was doing up there watching all that painting.

Insane is right.

Adam returned his head above Tommy's and realized that if someone looked on from the opposite direction, they'd look like a couple of Stooges performing some shenanigans. All they needed was Victor to join them and they'd have the third Stooge for their group.

The painting continued only for another minute or two as their father reached up and slapped a touch-up to the upper-right corner with a thin paintbrush. Then, he took a step back and checked the door from bottom to top and then back to the bottom. A few spots required another pop from the paintbrush and then everything seemed fine.

Their dad lowered the paintbrush into the tray and paused.

Adam and Tommy instinctively whipped back into hiding as hidden as they could be around the corner. Adam put his hand on Tommy's chest, holding him against the wall. They dared not move since the shuffling of their feet would give them away.

"Boys," their father said gruffly. "Are you watching me?"

Of course, they didn't answer.

"I know you're there. I heard you come up the stairs." He paused and Adam knew he hoped they would say something, to give him an excuse to make them get some *switchin'* sticks. "Okay then, if you don't want to admit you were standing in the hall *spying* on your good old dad, that's fine. I want you to listen to me for a minute." He let out a short laugh. "Stay silent if you agree to listen."

Something pounded the wall. "Yeah, that's what I thought," their father said. "As you shitbirds saw, I'm painting your dead mother's bedroom door golden—"

He didn't know why, but Adam tried to remember if *golden* was a color or if his father should have just said *gold.*

"—and it's very simple to understand. The door and the room behind it are off limits to you two. You are not to touch the door, mess with the door handle or even think about opening that door to go into the room. The door will be locked at all times and I painted the door golden to remind you to stay away from there."

Another pound slammed against the wall. Adam felt the vibration even on this perpendicular portion of the wall. He figured his dad was punching the wall for effect or intimidation.

Intimidation, of course. Why else would his father punch anything?

Their father continued: "So let's say one of you curious kitties get the inclination—"

Adam smiled; he didn't know his dad knew such a big word like *inclination*.

"—to check out the door. Let's say you either find the key, learn how to pick a lock or take the door off by the hinges. Now the bedroom is wide open for you to enter. You go in the room regardless of the golden color and the lock and my warnings. So this happens, right." Pause. "Do you little curious kitties know *then* what happens?"

Adam and Tommy already knew.

Another pound echoed through the barren hallways.

"I get angry," their father said, on the verge of yelling. "I get *very* angry because I told you not to go in there. You touched the door, broke the doorknob and entered the bedroom. You've no respect for your mother for doing that. You've no respect for me." Pause. "So in that case, *I* go out and pick a stick to *switch* you with. And believe me…"

A fourth pound, this one sounded like it cracked the wall, denting plaster. Their father's voice rose even more. "I will get the meanest, badass stick I can find! Something thick that doesn't bend when I smack your curious little kitty asses! *I will make sure that stick and you become real good friends!*"

Adam expected another punch, but instead all he heard was silence. His lifted his feet to the balls, ready to sprint down stairs if their father happened to come around the corner.

"So do you two understand what consequences there are if you actually do that?" His father asked, calmer.

Tommy started to step forward, probably to answer, but Adam tugged on his T-shirt. "No," Adam said, whispering into his brother's ear. "Don't."

"Good! I'm glad we have that understanding!" A footstep thumped and Adam was positive their father stood right around the corner. "Now, you have exactly ten seconds to leave this area. I don't care what you do: go to your rooms, go downstairs, or run out into the street. Just get the *fuck* away from this hallway! *Ten...*"

It only took the one second for Adam and Tommy to shuffle away. Adam didn't care if their footsteps clapped down the hall, onto the stairs and into the living room. Their father knew they were there and knew what they were doing. No sense in hiding it.

Adam heard his father say, "*Four!*" but they were safe on the couch. Safe in front of the television.

Safe as safe can be, Adam thought.

CHAPTER SIX

The Next Day

Near the end of July, the Youngstown Quarry immediately became busy since school started in two weeks and those who regretted letting the summer get away from them finally did something about it. When Adam and Tommy entered the quarry through the main entrance—a wooden gate attached to a nice wooden fence—they were met with outrageous shrills and screams of joy. Most of the quarry-goers were children, but a few parents strolled along the edges, staying far enough back from the water while staying close enough to keep an eye on their kids.

The quarry itself took up about half a block in either direction and at the deepest part, the water ran about twenty feet deep. Even up near the rock wall, the water was five or six feet deep. The park district had done a nice job in creating walkways around the quarry, as well as a fifty-foot dock that allowed those who cared to do so to launch small boats and rafts. Currently, two paddle boats, which could be rented at the store near the entrance, and a canoe, were the only craft in the quarry. On the few trees that could grow at the edge of the quarry, thick ropes hung for those daring enough to swing out into the water. Adam had done it many times and it's not as scary as some believed, though when he was seven or eight he probably felt he could die doing it.

"There are a lot of people here today," Tommy said.

"It's a hot day," Adam reasoned.

"The weather guy on TV said it is only going to get eighty-two degrees today. That's not that hot is it?"

"To some it is."

"Oh."

Tommy glanced around. "Do you see Reggie or Brenton?"

Adam gave a quick look around. "No, but I can't see who's on the other side."

"I'm going to go see," Tommy said.

"Did you forget something?"

Adam watched Tommy think for a moment and only remember when he saw what was in Adam's hand. "My life jacket?"

"Good answer."

Tommy couldn't swim, at least not well enough to manage in ten or twenty feet of water. He received free lessons from the park district and their neighbor gave them a child-size life jacket, which they took to the quarry anytime they wanted to go swimming. Adam helped the jacket open and Tommy slipped both hands in the holes. Kneeling, Adam ensured the straps were clipped, secured and tight.

"Is that too tight?" Adam asked.

"No."

"Okay. Don't leave the quarry."

"I won't."

"And if you're going to go into the deep section or swing off the ropes, come and get me so I can keep an eye on you."

Tommy laughed. "Are you my mother?"

As soon as the word mother came out, Tommy immediately stopped laughing. Adam started to laugh himself, but caught himself.

"I'm sorry," Tommy said, his voice on the verge of crying.

Adam put a reassuring hand on his brother's shoulder. "It's okay. You didn't mean anything bad by it." He gave him a shove. "Now go."

Tommy sprinted off, exuding the playfulness a nine-year-old should have. Adam watched his brother find one of his friends and they both went tumbling into the water. While Tommy wasn't afraid of the water—especially with a life jacket on—Adam still felt it prudent to monitor Tommy's actions because sometimes he got a little carried away. Once, last year, a different friend of his dared him to remove the jacket and swing over the water on the rope. Tommy took the dare and as Adam looked on, he knew from the start something didn't feel right. He couldn't explain the feeling: dread, implicit doom. Tommy snagged the rope from the hitch, placed one foot on the thick knot near the bottom and hopped up, pushing off the stone that was smooth on the side everyone used to push off. His brother floated over the edge, the shallow part of the quarry and then arced high over the deepest part of the water.

At that moment, his brother's hands began to slip and even though Tommy's feet appeared to remain solid on the knot, he had panicked. Afterwards, Adam consoled his brother, telling him that it was normal to panic, especially when he didn't know how to swim properly. The hands slipped and separated from the rope. This forced Tommy to fall backwards into the water. The twenty foot deep water. Combined with the ten or so foot drop from the rope and the swimming inexperience, Tommy didn't have a chance to right himself. On the way down, he turned slightly, but still entered the water parallel, the loud smack turning just about every head in the quarry that day.

As soon as Tommy hit the water, Adam was already diving from the edge. As he pumped his arms in and out of the water, Adam heard Tommy's wails and shrieks as he bobbed up and down in the water. He heard the splashing and he remembered the one thought as he made his way: *I never told him to be still if he ever thought he couldn't swim. I never told him to hold his breath and let his lungs raise him to the surface. That way, I'll have enough time to get to him.* But his brother kept flailing his arms and screaming.

It seemed like hours, the swim from the edge to Tommy. Hours that Adam thought for sure would do Tommy in. In actuality, Adam made the swim in less than fifteen seconds and just as Tommy sank into the water again, Adam looped an arm around his brother's armpit and hoisted him up enough so he could get some air.

"Take some air," he told Tommy. "Take some air and hang on."

The swim back took longer since Adam had his brother in tow. When they finally got to the edge, Adam pushed Tommy onto the rocks. Tommy rolled a few feet away and stayed there until he caught his breath. Adam lifted himself next to his brother and made sure Tommy was breathing properly.

"Never take your jacket off for anything," he said to Tommy, "until you can swim across the quarry on your own."

Tommy just nodded, spitting out quarry water. Soon after, that friend who dared Tommy into taking off the life jacket moved away, which Adam was grateful for. He never liked that kid.

But now, as he watched his brother splash water at his friends, Adam was positive that Tommy would think back to that moment the next time someone dared him to use that rope without a life jacket.

One of the volunteer lifeguards patrolled the far side of the quarry, where Tommy and his friend Paul stood. Since the quarry wasn't an official pool, the park district didn't officially employ any lifeguards. However, as small towns typically take care of their own, the volunteer lifeguards usually got a small stipend for their safety and work from the parents who were grateful to get their kids out of the house during the summer. The guards still had to be certified and maybe next year or the year after that when Adam hit his junior year he would try to become one.

As long as the lifeguard kept his eye on the kids, Adam could relax. He sat down on the rocky edge and dangled his feet into the water. The quarry water couldn't be more than seventy degrees or so. He'd get in eventually and work his body into the water, starting with his feet.

"Adam!" He heard someone call behind him.

He turned and saw Victor running across the edge, his feet flapping against the rocks, splattering water in small eruptions around his feet.

"Victor! What's up?"

From across the quarry, the lifeguard yelled, "No running Victor!"

He slowed, but it was only another couple of steps anyway.

"How long have you been here?" Adam asked.

Victor shrugged. "An hour or so." He pointed to the left, to a group of six girls congregating around blankets and picnic baskets. "Violet's here. You should go say hi."

"Not in the mood."

"You're never in the mood. She likes you, you know."

Adam looked over at Violet. She wore a two-piece red bathing suit and pink water slippers. Her black hair, wet from a recent swim, hung in strings down to the top of her breasts, which had developed into a head start over the other girls. He imagined the ends of the hair tickling her skin as she talked and laughed and moved her head around. The hair framed her round face in a way a picture is inserted into the right picture frame. These thoughts made his stomach jump.

"So you say," Adam said.

"So does everyone say."

Violet caught Adam's eye and smiled. She gave him a slight wave. The surrounding girls followed her wave and starting giggling, holding their mouths and then telling each other things in whispers. Violet nodded in answer to a girl's question, and then all six of them rose and jumped into the water.

"Well, if you don't do something about it, Chambers is going to get her."

Adam nodded. "I know…"

Victor sat down next to Adam and plopped his own feet into the water. "You need to get out of your little funk. It's the summer!"

Smiling, Adam said, "There's not much that will get me out of the funk."

"Maybe Violet could."

"Funny—"

"A little kiss might do you wonders."

Violet had broken away from her friends and was talking to two other girls Adam didn't recognize.

"At the minimum," Adam said as he felt Victor's head moving around to look him eye to eye. "What?"

"Something's wrong. Spill it."

Adam looked at Tommy, who was sticking close to the edge. Tommy's friend was splashing water on Tommy and another boy and they were all laughing. "Well," Adam said, "last night I saw my dad doing the strangest thing."

"Only last night, huh?"

"Quiet, I'm trying to tell you."

"Sorry."

"Tommy kept bugging me to play catch at the park and I didn't really want to. Finally, I said yes and Tommy tossed the baseball pretty hard at me. I couldn't catch it and it went upstairs. When we went to get it, we heard these weird noises coming from the hallway. You remember where my parents' bedroom used to be?" Adam had taken Victor in that bedroom a few times because it had the best view onto the street when they threw water balloons at people walking by.

Victor nodded.

"My father was painting that door gold," Adam finished.

"What? Why was he painting it?"

"I don't know. He said we would get it big trouble if we went in there."

"Did you go in there?"

Adam gave Victor a quizzical look. "Do you think I want to get switched? Besides, it's locked and I don't know where he'd keep the key."

"What do you think is in there?"

"Probably something he doesn't want me or Tommy to see."

"Of course. Why so much trouble, right?"

"Yeah, he sounded really into it."

Victor grunted a little noise and peered into the distance. Adam couldn't tell what he was looking at, but Adam recognized the posture and gaze as thoughtful. When Victor had this look on him, Adam left him alone.

In larger clusters, clouds graced the sky, moving slowly in front of the sun. Shade started to cover the quarry, with little patches of sunlight forcing its way to the water. Each time the sun went hidden, Adam felt the temperature drop a few degrees before rising again when the sun reappeared. This was, as his mother would say, *a perfect and most beautiful day*. She would say it with her eyes closed, looking up to the sky, as if praying to God. Maybe she was praying to God as she said it, in thanks for bringing this day. His mother tried to bring religion into their lives, but their father didn't care enough to support it. Attending church was irregular, but they always went on Easter, Thanksgiving and Christmas, whether his father allowed it or not.

"You must go in there," he thought he heard Victor say.

"What?"

"There's only one thing you have to do and that's to see what Joe doesn't want you to see."

"And get in trouble."

"Hey, I didn't say you wouldn't get in trouble, but don't you want to know why he painted that door gold?"

"Sure, but—"

"If ifs and buts were candy and nuts, we'd all be trick-or-treating." Victor's eyes went wide; an idea struck him. "We'll all go in there. You, me and Tommy. Three of us."

"I don't know…"

"It's settled."

A pattering of feet stomped up behind them. Adam whipped around, seeing Tommy, who said, "What's settled?"

"Nothing," Adam said.

"Did you tell Victor about the door?"

Adam sighed. He didn't want Tommy involved. When the time came, only Victor and Adam would go beyond the door. No Tommy. No need for him to go also.

"Yes sir," Victor said. "He told me and I suggested we all go and see what's behind the door."

"Can we?" Tommy pleaded. "Please, Adam?"

Victor shook Adam. "Yeah, Adam, can we?" Victor smirked, already knowing the answer. When Adam didn't answer, Victor said, "We shall take that as a yes, Tommy!"

Both of their cheers drew some attention, which embarrassed Adam. There was no need to act how they were; it's not like they won the lottery or got the big gift for Christmas. Water splashed on his leg. Adam looked down and saw Violet treading towards him. She threw more water on him.

"Hey, Adam."

"Hey."

Victor tugged at Tommy. "Let's go little guy. I want to throw you in the water."

"Push me on the swing really hard. I want to fly high." Tommy took off running towards the closest swing before someone claimed it.

Victor smiled and sarcastically saluted Adam. "Have fun kids." He followed Tommy to the swing.

"How are you," Violet asked.

"I'm good."

"Are you sad summer's almost over?"

"A little. I like school though."

She smiled. "Even as a freshman?"

"Well, it's all school to me."

Violet leaned on the rocks and propped her head on her forearms. She moved her elbows close to Adam's thigh—which he figured might be on purpose—and said, "I'm sorry about your mom."

Adam shrugged. He was getting used to people still saying "sorry about your mom" or "my condolences" or "my prayers are with you." Mostly, those phrases came from people he didn't know; sometimes people just said those things because they didn't know what else to say. A few of his mother's friends worked at the school and even though they said the same things, Adam knew they meant them more than anyone. With Violet he wasn't so sure. She started talking to him at the end of last school year, but they've never really hung out or had long conversations about anything. And now with her *I'm sorry about your mom*, she suddenly took the next step into friendship.

"Thank you," Adam said, responding the only way he knew how and the only way he had been responding since the funeral.

"Have you done anything fun? Did you go on vacation anywhere yet?"

Shaking his head, Adam said, "No and no."

"What have you been doing?"

"Reading. Riding my bike. Stuff like that."

"Doesn't sound too exciting," Violet murmured.

"Yeah, well, not that much of a chance to do anything exciting."

"Oh." Violet now looked uncomfortable. She moved away, looking around for her friends. "What are you plans for the rest of the summer?"

Now her questions sound like small talk, just something to get through the next minute or so until she found an excuse to break away.

"I don't know," Adam answered. "Haven't really thought about it."

Violet's head locked on to her friends, who were congregating at the furthest tree swing from them. "If you feel like hanging out, let me know. You know where I live?"

Adam nodded.

"Good. Just drop by or something. I'll be a bike riding partner for you."

"Okay."

"I mean it. We could ride down County Line road and check out that abandoned house or something."

"Yeah, maybe."

"It's supposed to be haunted. I think people think any abandoned house is haunted."

Adam nodded. "Probably."

Violet smiled. "Man of a few syllables. No one can say you're long-winded." She looked up at him and Adam thought her eyes were going to stop his heart. "Don't forget to drop by. Thursdays are the best day until school."

She turned towards him, her long hair flowing over his thighs. It was accidental, but his flesh turned to immediate goosebumps. The hairs at the base of his neck came to life and put shivers down his spine. Adam liked that feeling and he quickly saddened when Violet pushed off the rock wall with her legs and swam away.

As soon as Violet was a few feet away, Victor and Tommy returned.

"So," Victor said. "You guys boyfriend and girlfriend?"

"No, jerk. She just wanted to know about my summer."

"Right." Victor mocked. To Tommy, he said, "Looks like your brother has a girlfriend."

Tommy chuckled. "You going to marry her Adam?"

Despite being the butt in his friend and brother's joke, Adam wished the summer stayed like this day. His brother laughing and outgoing and Victor showcasing his greatest skill: being a friend. The weather couldn't have been more perfect and Adam remembered what his mother would say on perfect days like this: "Adam, God gives us the sunshine so we can bask in His creation; He gives us air so we can breathe and bask in the presence of each other." Sometimes his mom use to say the strangest things, but that phrase was beautiful to him. It came down to love, he knew. Love God and love each other. He had to figure that one out on his own; his mother warned him after she said it she wasn't going to tell him the meaning of her words. It took Adam a few days, but when he understood what his mom meant, he vowed to never forget to bask in His creation when there's sunshine and bask in each other when there's air, which meant all the time.

So today he basked both in the sunshine and enjoyed breathing the air with Tommy and Victor.

They left the park a short time later: Tommy's legs and arms rubbery from the constant swimming and Adam's abdomen tight and sore from the welcomed laughing from Victor's cajoling and bad jokes.

Hey Adam, what do termites eat for breakfast? I don't know what? Dramatic pause from Victor. OAKMEAL!

Through the gate, Adam still thought *oakmeal* was funny. He'd have to tell Violet that one, if he decided to go on that bike ride.

He smiled to himself; he probably would.

CHAPTER SEVEN

The Following Morning

A door slammed, jolting Adam awake.

The clock on his nightstand read 8:19 A.M. He rubbed his eyes until the gooey sleepers left. Looking over, he saw his brother still sleeping, the rise and fall of the Spider-man blanket following each breath. He threw both feet out of the bed to the floor, glad he still had on socks because he knew the wood floor would be ice cold. Adam crept past his brother's bed to the window, just in time to see his father getting into his beat-up red truck.

The truck, long overdue for an oil change, sputtered to life, kicking back a puff of smoke from the muffler. Adam heard the transmission grind into first gear—which was also probably long overdue for repairs—and eased the truck into the street. Seconds later, the truck and his father turned a corner and were gone.

"Was that dad?" Tommy asked sleepily.

"Yeah."

"Where's he going?"

"Don't know. He didn't let us know."

Adam saw Tommy's brain kick-start. "Call Victor! Now's the perfect chance!" His brother blurted.

"We don't know when he's going to be back. By the time Victor gets over here, dad might return."

Tommy slammed back down in the bed. "Victor said you'd make excuses."

"I don't want to get caught. You know what will happen if we do."

"If you don't call him, *I will*!"

Adam grabbed the cordless phone. "Fine! But *you* are not going in there. Just me and Victor." He quickly dialed Victor's number before Tommy could protest.

Victor's mother answered and was surprised Adam was calling so early, she'd have to wake him up.

"Hello?" Victor mumbled.

"Hey. It's Adam."

"Why are you calling so early?"

"My dad's gone."

A pause on the other end. "Really?"

"You still want to do this? Tommy is ready."

"Yeah. I'm leaving as soon as I hang up the phone. See ya."

As the handset docked with the base, Tommy asked, "So is he coming?"

"Yes. He'll be here as quick as he can." Adam went to his dresser and selected jeans and a T-shirt to wear for the day. A shower could wait. It would probably be weird if Victor got here when he was in the shower. "You should get dressed before he gets here."

Tommy's covers flew off the bed and he hopped to his own dresser to find some clothes.

"And brush your teeth."

"Adam, why? I'm too excited."

"Excitement doesn't brush your teeth: the toothbrush does."

In minutes both of them were fully dressed. Tommy disappeared to hopefully brush his teeth. The Blow Test—when Adam had Tommy blow his breath in Adam's face—would determine if his brother truly brushed his teeth or just ran a wet brush in his mouth. It comforted Adam to see Tommy acting like an actual kid this morning and yesterday and he hoped their little adventure continued that attitude.

Adam stood by the window again. A dreary day surrounded the house. Low-lying rain clouds hovered unmoving in the sky, ready to pelt the ground with rain. On days like today, his mother would say, "It's okay to cry sometimes because even God cries." He looked up, trying to find an opening in the clouds, but gave up after a few seconds. It would have to be rain today, he guessed. Good thing they were staying indoors. Maybe later, if the weather improved, he'd take Tommy to the park and they could practice catching, and maybe some hitting.

The street held no activity this morning and Adam figured everyone who had a regular job already left this morning. If anyone looked on when his dad left, they might think he had a regular job. That in itself sounded like the punchline to a silly joke. *Who knows where Adam's dad was going! Is it a) the bar; b) to look for a job; or c) the bar!* Adam tried to remember the last time he saw his dad out this early and he went back to the time before the accident. His father usually rose at 6:30 and headed out the door by 7:00 so he could start work at 7:30. At that time, Adam and Tommy's mother would wake them, with breakfast already made (unless it was cereal, then all she did was slice bananas or sprinkle blueberries on the corn flakes) and their lunches ready to go. Everybody was up and everybody was doing their things.

After the accident, his father woke up later and later and many times, his mother tried to get him up when they got up for school, but she usually failed. All his father wanted to do was lie around until noon and then get up, grab a beer and go to the shed. Adam, Tommy and their mother knew he had a small fridge he salvaged from someone's junk one day and kept unknown quantities of beer in it. Sometimes he'd leave the shed and disappear for hours and no one would really know. Adam wondered if time was irrelevant to his father as he let each minute slip away in beer, cursing and *switchin'*.

The faucet shut off in the bathroom and Adam heard the toilet flush. Tommy returned a minute later and asked, "Do you want me to do The Blow Test?"

"Sure." Adam knelt down and Tommy released a thick breath. The mint smell rushed up Adam's nose, almost making him sneeze. "Smells good."

"Wait 'til I eat onion for breakfast."

"Funny."

"Do you see Victor yet?"

Adam pressed his face against the window and saw Victor rapidly peddling his bike into the driveway. "He just pulled in."

Tommy dashed out of the room, his footsteps thumping down the stairs seconds later. Before Adam could even reach the landing, he heard the front door open and Tommy saying, "Hey Victor!"

As Adam stood halfway down the stairs, Victor threw him a wave. "You ready to go?"

"Of course he is," Tommy answered instead. "He's ready."

Victor lightly rubbed Tommy's hair. "I think you're more ready than anyone." To Adam he said, "Is this the first fun thing you guys have done all summer?"

"Besides baseball, yes." Tommy tugged at Victor's arms.

Adam completed coming down the stairs and pulled Tommy's arm away. "Tommy, don't be annoying."

"We should check it out as soon as possible," he said to Victor. "We don't know when our dad's coming back. He left about ten minutes ago."

"Where do you think he went?" Victor asked.

"This early? No clue."

Victor pulled a flashlight from his back pocket and a black gun. Tommy jumped back, his eyes enlarging. Adam stepped between the gun and Tommy. "What are you doing with that?" Adam said, concerned.

"Aw, don't worry. It's just a BB gun." Victor slid the bolt clamp back. There was a click and a snap as the clamp whipped back into place.

"It's still a gun."

"BBs don't hurt all that much."

"I don't care," Adam said firmly. "Put it back in your pocket."

"Fine." His friend switched the safety on and tucked the BB gun back into his pocket. "Ready?"

Adam led Victor and Tommy up the stairs and into the hall before the door.

The golden door held its sheen well, drying impressively. His father's meticulous painting covered every inch of the door, including the area around the hinges and the doorknob. The trim that went around the door about two or three inches inward was also painted gold, but it appeared to have faded a little in the two days since the original coatings. This was the first time Adam or Tommy had been in the hallway leading directly to the door and right at that moment, Adam felt as if he were by himself. No Tommy; no Victor; quite possibly, not even himself. He knew he was standing here, but was he feeling like he existed here? His thoughts shot around his brain like lightning bolts and he tried to rein them in but they continued to elude any process of containment. He knew he needed to move his foot forward to take a step, but his limbs felt detached, not even his. In his immobility, the door mocked him: *Hey Adam. Do you like how your dad painted me? Like the color? I do. It reminds me of the punishment you'll receive if you cross me. Get it? Cross me? I knew you'd come, Adam. I knew you couldn't resist seeing what's behind me. And let me tell you. It's a doozy. You're going to* love *what's behind door number one. You don't need any other doors but me.*

Adam closed his eyes, but his mind still saw the door.

I see you've brought some friends. Now that is perfect. The more the merrier, right Adam? You were never one for large crowds. Heck, I don't even think you're even one for friends. You had to bring your brother, though; nice touch. You should have brought more people, but you three will have to do. I'm hungry Adam; it's time to feed me.

"Stop it," Adam said as quietly as he could.

"What?" Victor and Tommy said together.

"I said do you guys feel that?" He asked Victor and Tommy.

"Feel what?" Victor answered.

"I don't know. I can't describe it exactly."

"All I feel is you stalling."

Adam finally took a step towards the door. The air pressed down on him and he wanted to sit down and let the strangeness pass, but he knew Victor or Tommy would raze him. Besides, the slower he took, the more time he allowed for his father to return. Each step took large amounts of effort, but all three finally reached the door.

Without hesitation, Tommy extended his hand for the doorknob.

"Don't!" Adam snapped.

"Why not?" Tommy drew his hand back and looked at the door as if it had teeth.

"Wet paint."

Victor laughed. "Your father didn't paint the doorknob. No wet paint there." Victor grabbed onto the knob. "I'll go first since your father can't really punish me."

"No," Adam said, "but we'll get the consequences for *your* actions."

As soon as Victor twisted the knob, a deep guttural growl wafted through the door. It was short, but very effective in forcing Victor to pull away.

"You guys get a dog?"

Tommy shook his head and Adam said, "Don't you think I would have told you?"

Another growl came, and it slowly rose into a whispered shriek. The sound impaled their ears, causing all three to plug their ears with fingers. Even with that protection, Adam still heard the thin, sharp needlepoint scream. The doorknob vibrated and then everything went silent. The boys lowered their hands.

"Okay," Victor said. "I believe you don't have a dog."

"We have to tell our dad," Tommy said.

"No way," Victor said. "You'll get in trouble because then he'll *know* you were in there." He shook his head. "We have to find out ourselves."

Adam started to push his brother and Victor away from the door. "No we don't."

Holding his ground, Victor said, "You've been watching too many scary movies. What could be in there? Maybe your dad left the TV on. Maybe your dad *did* get a dog and doesn't want you to know."

"Both crazy ideas."

"Adam, where's your sense of adventure?"

"Downstairs on the couch and away from this door and far away from any punishment from my dad."

Victor scoffed. Adam didn't like the scoffing Victor. This Victor was aggressive and selfish. This Victor needed a *switchin'* or an attitude adjustment. Or both. When Victor replaced his hand on the doorknob, Adam stepped back, pulling Tommy with him.

The doorknob slowly turned in Victor's hand. The small gears inside the handle pulled the rod, easing it inside the door. When the handle turned no further, Victor pushed the door slightly inward. The edge of the door broke free from the jamb, creating an inch of clearance. Victor looked back and smiled. "It's fine." He opened the door a little more.

Adam didn't know what he expected from any of Victor's actions. Really, all his friend could do was open the door and go inside, but as he watched Victor push the door open and look back at him, Adam thought for a moment everything was going to be just fine. That everything would be like yesterday's perfect day. Sunny, carefree, jovial. *Jovial is a good word*, Adam thought. *Jovial is for Santa Claus or laughing too hard at a bad and silly joke at the same time. Jovial is for the last day of school. Jovial is also for the first day of school. Jovial is also for a first kiss. Jovial is for the feeling of being with mother. Jovial is not for this situation.* But why would he think that? No light spilled from the room; strange sounds were inside; and Victor was relentless in his quest to see inside the bedroom.

Something shifted inside. Something heavy and lumbering. A rumble shook the door and Victor released the handle. A growl erupted too close to the door like when the TV's volume was extremely loud when it's shut off and when it's turned back on the sound blasts through the room.

"Victor," Adam calmly said. "Get away from there."

Adam saw in his eyes that Victor wanted to, but something deeper kept him at the door, pushing the door inward even more. Was it the curiosity of the sound? The movement? Tommy latched on to Adam's shirt and tugged.

"Come on Adam, make him come back," Tommy said, his voice trembling.

"I'm trying."

"I don't like this."

"Well, you should have thought about that before you got all reckless."

"*I'm scared!*" Tommy half-whispered, half-yelled.

"*Tommy*." Adam said. "Let the door go. We should go downstairs."

What would Victor think of him if he just took Tommy right now and went downstairs? He could just say he was protecting Tommy, getting out of a frightening situation. Would Victor believe it or would he just use the moment to mock Adam and possibly even his brother? This Victor wasn't the Victor Adam wanted to be friends with.

Victor turned and finally said, "It's just a damn door you Shaws. Now get up here with me and let's get inside."

"*No, Adam, don't.*" Tommy said.

"I'm not, but I have to take a few steps to get him." Adam held his brother's right hand. "That okay?"

Tommy nodded.

Adam reached out to take Victor's collar, but something inside the room was much, much faster.

A meaty hand, fingers as thick as burnt sausages, gripped the side of the door. The fingers curled one at a time around the edge, just a few inches above the strikeplate. Victor seemed oblivious to the hand because he turned back to Adam and beckoned for him to follow. Adam shook his head and pointed.

Too late.

The door whipped open so fast Adam's eyes lagged, missing the moment the door crashed into an inner wall. The hand came out farther, followed by a forearm caked with bulging blue veins. They rose from the skin, pulsating blood through whatever the arm connected to. The light surrounded the crack, but *disappeared* when it crossed the threshold of the door. *How could light disappear?* Adam shot a look at the hall window to verify that it was still daylight outside and then looked back into the room. Still dark. In fact, Adam could see nothing inside the bedroom. Just blackness. He knew the one window in the bedroom was directly across from the door, but no light came in. It's possible the curtains were drawn; however, even then, some light would get through.

"*Wha*—"Victor managed to say before the bulky hand clasped onto his neck.

"Victor!" Adam dove forward and latched onto his friend's belt. His grip was weak; the top third of his index, middle and ring finger only hooked the belt. Behind him, Tommy cowered against the wall. "Tommy! Go into the other hall! Stay there!"

He watched Tommy disappear around the corner and then heard footsteps on the stairs. Even better.

From the bedroom, the most chopped up, beastly roar shot out from the dark recesses of the house. *Mrrrrraaaaarrrrrr!* Like the same movement from the wave at a baseball game, Adam felt the sound's vibrations emanating from the arm to Victor, through his belt and up Adam's arm. The throbbing was too strong and Adam had to let go of Victor's belt. With methodical jerks, the beastly hand pulled Victor into the room.

"Adam! Pull me out!" Victor tried to break free. He couldn't. "I can't get away! *I can't get away!*" Victor planted his feet just as Adam put his arms around his friend's waist. Another foot and both of them would be inside the room.

With a force he never drummed up before, Adam pulled with all his might. He felt nothing give, so he tried again and for a second he thought he heard Victor's feet slide back.

"Yes," Victor said, confirming the progression. "Yes! Keep going!"

Again, Adam used all his strength and this time he was positive they were both moving backwards now even though he felt the tugging from the other way. Victor placed a foot on the six-inch piece of wall jutting out on the right and pushed into Adam.

Mrrrrrrraaaaaaaaaaaaaaaaaaaaaaar!

They were making it! They were actually making it! Adam held his friend tight, just like when he pulled Tommy from the quarry last year.

"Adam! On three pull as hard as you can!"

Adam grabbed each forearm with the opposite hand and squeezed tight. Victor bent his right leg.

"One…"

The arm pulled harder and harder, as if knowing Victor's plan.

"Two…"

The strength flowing through Adam grew quickly in anticipation of the next number.

"*Three!*"

Both boys pushed and pulled at the same time with equal strength. The monster hand released and they went tumbling back, Victor on top of Adam. Victor rolled to the side, propped himself on his knees and clapped Adam on his legs.

"Thank you!" He pointed behind him. "Did you see that? The hand; the arm?"

"Yes. We need to get out of here and tell my father."

"Maybe not him," Victor said. "The police, someone else, but not your dad."

"Let's get Tommy and go."

Victor stood. Before he took one step, a plump blob shot from the darkness of the bedroom and wrapped its arms around Tommy in a bear hug, trapping both arms to Victor's side. He twisted and shimmied; the hold was too tight.

"Adam! It's got me again!"

Whatever it was limped backwards, taking Victor with him. Adam could see the thing's legs, stubby and very powerful, with horrendous and hairy sores oozing blood or puss or a combination of both. Some bile started to come up as Adam's stomach lurched.

The thing growled, confirming the hands and arms and the growls earlier were from this beast as well. Victor struggled harder and he looked at Adam, his eyes defeated and realizing that something bad was going to happen. And it did. The beast slacked its grip and before Victor could make any movement otherwise, one of the thing's hands grabbed onto Victor's forearm and ripped the entire arm from the socket. Adam cringed as blood splattered the walls and the bone cracked free. It sounded like a sheet of paper being ripped longwise and then an axe splitting a stump of wood.

Victor screamed in extreme agony. He dropped to his knees, strings of muscle and skin slapping the area around the wound. Victor's face scrunched until Adam thought it would implode on itself. As Victor dropped to the floor, the face of the beast appeared.

It had long, black stringy hair. More sores on the face and a partial nose. The skin had a tint of green-brown. The face's shape was all the shapes rolled into one: round, sharp angles, slanted cheek bones and triangle-like ears. All the shapes kids learned in grade school. The thing smiled, exposing normal human teeth, though some were missing.

The thing held up Victor's arm, opened its mouth wide—wider than any normal person or animal should—and stuck the bloody end of the arm into the gap. The monster chewed the arm bit by bit until it reached the elbow. Blood dripped from its mouth; tendons hung grossly from its lips. Then, it tossed the arm through the door, the bedroom swallowing Victor's arm as the beast did.

Another second later, it maneuvered around Victor and started shoving him into the bedroom. With each push, a grunt of effort. With each grunt of effort, a sickening rub of Victor's flesh against the wooden floor. *Swwwwwit*, grunt, *Swwwwwit,* grunt, *Swwwwwit*. Adam thought the sounds would go on forever and knew he should stop the thing, but he remained frozen on the floor, watching his friend vanish into the bedroom, the dark swallowing him with ease.

The monster also disappeared into the dark, but popped its head out and gazed at Adam, who scooted backwards until he hit the wall. The thing's eyes widened, as in surprise, and raised a hand to grip the door handle. Adam continued to push against the wall, thinking he was next, that his arm would be ripped from his body and chewed on like beef jerky.

But none of that happened. The thing stepped back and quietly shut the door.

Adam still couldn't move. He still heard sounds coming from the bedroom. First, the *Swwwwwit,* grunt, *Swwwwwit,* grunt occurred again, though somewhat muted. Then, another block of ripping sounds, accompanied by Victor's intense screams. After a minute,

Victor's cries slowly diminished until all Adam heard was what he could assume was the beast's eating.

Worse, Adam thought the monster *dined* on Victor. He envisioned a small table, or possibly a lap tray since he figured the thing slept on his mother's bed, with a plate and the proper silverware settings and a fancy cloth napkin built into a cone like those restaurants that have appetizers for $30, and a half-full wine glass. A butler would stroll by with a serving tray and would set it on the nightstand saying *and tonight's main course is...Adam's friend! He's served with a thick blood sauce and a side of muscle-meat and optional epidermal slices.*

Adam leaned over and threw up a stream of hot bile. A stream of saliva hung from the corner of his mouth as he planted his face directly onto the floor. A rising blubber found its way out and with it, a few moments of tears.

His throat ached and his gag reflex wanted to do it again but a swallow calmed it all down. Adam lifted himself up and checked the bedroom door. It was still shut, the golden color teasing him, begging him to just come right on up and open it. *There's nothing to be afraid of. It might be dark inside, but there's nothing inside. Just the dark and...oh wait, Victor's in there. You want to come in and get him? I'm sure he wants you to join him, maybe play a nice game of Chess or Battleship. Nope, that's right, he's been eaten.*

Adam raised his weak legs. He had to hold himself up with the wall as he made his way to the staircase.

"Tommy?" He attempted to say. His voice wouldn't come through his bile-lined throat very well. He tried again. "Tommy?" It came out better this time. "Where are you?"

He didn't receive an answer.

The stairs below him seemed to go on forever. Like Frodo's trip to Mount Doom. On and on. Adam's first step was solid and he quickly gained more confidence as he lumbered through each step.

By the time he reached the bottom, the strength in his legs returned.

"Tommy?"

He walked down the first floor hallway looking into the living room and the front room. After opening the front door and checking the yard, he headed for the kitchen. He peered through the back door window and saw Tommy sitting by the large oak tree, his knees drawn to his chest.

Adam opened the door and ran to his brother.

"Tommy, are you alright?"

Tommy looked the other way, near the end of a huge crying fit. "What was that? What was that *thing?*" His voice still held hints of the recent cry.

"I don't know, Tommy. I don't know."

"Is it gone?"

"No. It went back into the bedroom."

"I want it gone." Tommy hoisted himself up and hugged Adam. In Adam's shirt, Tommy said, "Did it get Victor?"

Adam didn't want to answer the question; he couldn't answer the question. Of course, the answer was yes, but did it all really happen? Did his friend really get his arm ripped off by a fat beast that came from his dead mother's bedroom?

"Yes, Tommy. It got Victor."

Tommy backed away. "*Why didn't you stop it? Why didn't you stop it from getting Victor?*"

"I tried. I tried!" Adam's eyes welled immensely, sadness boiling into his head. It had to go somewhere, and it left through his eyes. Through his soft wails, Adam said, "I tried, Tommy. I tried but I wasn't strong enough."

"We have to tell dad." Tommy wiped his eyes and stood up all the way. "Dad needs to know."

Adam shook his head. "There is no way we can tell dad."

Tommy looked up at him, disappointment shining into Adam's body. "Why?"

"Do I really need to tell you?"

"Yes, tell me." His brother's voice deepened, as if he had matured thirty years. Adam heard wisdom and intelligence behind those three words and it scared him.

"Want to pick a branch right now? Have it ready for when he comes home and we tell him? If he finds out we went anywhere *near* that door, let alone opened it for that...for that *monster* so it could get Victor, he will *switch* us until we bleed." Adam cupped Tommy's chin. "*How's that for telling you.*"

"But Victor's dead."

Calming down, Adam said, "I know. Give me some time to figure that out." He saw Tommy's doubt. "I promise."

"Okay."

"There's something we need to do and I know you won't like it."

"What is it?"

"We have to go up there and clean up the hallway."

"But his *blood* is there."

"I know, Tommy. It has to be done and quickly."

Adam started towards the house and heard Tommy follow him. When he reached the door, Adam turned back: Tommy was peering up at something.

"What are you looking at?" Adam asked him.

Tommy just pointed.

Adam came back down from the back steps and stood next to Tommy, following his gaze.

Immediately, he knew it was the second floor window to his mother's bedroom. Adam was right earlier when he guessed the curtains *weren't* drawn: he could see the outline of them on each side of the window. The problem wasn't the curtains or the window itself or anything around the window, it was the other side of the window. The same darkness could be seen from this side as it looked when he was in the hallway. Deep, threatening darkness, waiting to gorge on anything that entered it. Adam found the other windows on the house—whether on the first or second floor—allowed the morning light inside. Adam couldn't make out anything in the bedroom even though he knew a shoulder-high dresser sat directly to the right of the window. Sometimes, when playing in the back yard, he could see some of the top of the dresser poking into view.

"How is it doing that?" Tommy asked. "All that dark?"

Adam shrugged.

"Do you think dad knows?"

"Maybe," Adam said. "Maybe not." But if Adam had to place money on the maybe and maybe not, he'd bet everything on the maybe.

CHAPTER EIGHT

Three hours later.

It was unheard of for their dad to be gone for four hours. Sometimes he'd come and go or sometimes he'd just hang out in the shed. Regardless, he always came home at random times for who knows how long. But it seemed to never go longer than an hour. It's like their dad had an internal alarm clock that went off every hour, bleeping, *Hey Joe, it's time to head back to the house and see what your little shitbirds are doing.* And he'd answer, *Very true. They're probably eating dinner without me or making a mess of something.*

Adam was glad, though, that he and Tommy had three hours to clean up the mess in the hallway. They took a gamble, hoping their dad wouldn't come back and that gamble paid off.

The blood on the walls was the toughest part. A simple mop took care of the blood on the hardwood floors and the vacuum sucked up any chunks of flesh or other pieces of Victor's arm that fell to the side. Once,

Tommy puked and the vacuum made quick work of even that mess. Adam smartly emptied the vacuum canister into the metal trash can by the shed and rinsed the mop out with the garden hose. The only problem that remained was the blood smell. That tinge of metallic smell hovered in the air just enough to cause concern for Adam and his brother. Adam thought bleach might do the trick, but then the bleach would be suspicious and on all the TV shows and movies, the bleach always got someone in trouble. Adam did *not* want to get in trouble and did not want the bleach to do it.

Tommy suggested they spray some of their dad's deodorant in the hallway and just say they used it when they took showers. It wasn't a bad plan and that's what they went with, spraying the aerosol can for about thirty seconds before they felt satisfied they couldn't smell the blood.

"I think we've done a good job here," Adam said. "Now promise me this stays between us until I can figure out what to do."

Tommy glanced from the golden door to Adam and back to the door. Adam still sense some doubt in his brother. "I promise," Tommy said. "But please figure something out fast. That room scares me."

"Me too."

A truck rumbled into the driveway. Adam and Tommy stood there like statues, losing any thought on what they should do next.

"To our room," Adam suggested.

Tommy nodded and walked into their room, plopping on the bed and grabbing a book from the nightstand.

"Really read," he told Tommy. "Don't pretend to read the book. You'll make it obvious."

"Okay."

The truck door slammed. Adam stood at the window, to the side, peering down at his dad.

His father went to the bed of the truck and dropped the tailgate. He hopped into the rusty and mud-caked bottom. From up in his bedroom, Adam heard the shocks groan madly. Then he bent over and tried to dead-lift a garbage bag that bulged with something lumpy. His dad struggled with the bulky thing and Adam seriously considered pulling up the window and asking if he could use any help. How stupid would that be? His father would know that he was being spied on and he'd probably not be pleased.

A minute later, Joe rolled the garbage bag to the end of the truck bed and gave it one last heave to force it to the ground. He jumped to the ground and went around the corner of the shed. He soon came back with a large dolly.

"Where did he get that?" Adam said aloud.

"What?"

"Nothing. Thinking out loud."

He'd never seen that dolly before, neither in the shed nor in the yard, but here was his dad wheeling the thing right up to the black garbage bag. His dad worked the flat bottom of the dolly under the bag and unwound a strap from the middle of the back part. After wrapping the strap around the bag, he tightened the wench, which returned most of the strap to the spool. Then, his dad flipped down a small set of wheels on a bar and used all of his weight to tilt the entire contraption towards him. The dolly was meant to wheel things as heavy as or much, much heavier than the garbage bag. Turning the dolly, his father effortlessly pushed the dolly and the garbage bag towards the house.

Soon, everything left Adam's sight and soon after that, the outside cellar doors creaked open and the dolly banged rhythmically as it maneuvered down the cellar stairs, once step at a time.

Bloomp...bloomp...bloomp...bloomp.

"Was that dad?" Tommy asked.

"Yes."

"What is he doing?"

"Not sure. Go back to your book." Tommy did.

Adam stepped out into the hallway and tried to see down the stairs, to see anything that would give him a clue to his dad's antics. What was in the bag? Where was he all morning? Did his whereabouts and that bag have something in common? And finally, why did he take the mysterious bag to the cellar?

He wouldn't worry about that for the moment. The first thing he had to think about was if his dad would notice anything out of place in the hallway by the bedroom door. The one good thing, if it could be called a good thing, was his dad had no idea that Victor had come over this morning.

Victor's dead, you know, his mind recalled.

I know.

He was your best friend, Adam.

I know.

Your only friend, Adam.

He didn't want to think so, but he still told himself, *I know.*

Hey Adam, his mind serenely said. *Do you think your dad will see Victor's bike in the front yard?*

"Shit," Adam blurted.

"What?" Tommy sat up.

"I've got to hide Victor's bike."

Extreme doom covered Tommy's face. In an instant, his face became pale, fearful of their dad discovering the bike.

"Come on," Adam pleaded as he dashed from the bedroom.

As they bounced down the stairs, Adam said, "Stay by the kitchen door and listen for dad coming up from cellar."

"What are you going to do with the bike?"

Adam shook his head. He had no idea so there was no since in hiding that face from Tommy. "I'll figure it out. Just make some noise, like you're playing Army or something if you hear dad."

"Okay. Army."

Adam bolted through the front door and saw Victor's blue 10-speed—an actual racing back like they used in the Tour de France—lying carelessly in the yard. It was a nice bike; Adam would have given anything to have such a nice bike. Now was his chance, but deep down Adam couldn't claim ownership of his best friend's bike. Not now. Not ever.

He pulled the bike upright and looked around. In his field of vision, no spot appeared convenient or seemed like it would hide the bike well. He could dump the bike in a neighbor's yard, but any place close to the house would probably elicit suspicion. Besides, what reasons would Victor have to leave his bike in a neighbor's yard?

The park might be a good spot. He could ride the bike there in less than five minutes and run back in less than ten. A quick calculation brought the total time to around ten to fifteen minutes. Adam didn't think he had that much time. Adam had to assume that whatever his dad was doing in the cellar would take another minute or two.

Panic started in Adam's feet. A strange coldness told Adam that there was no answer to the bike problem. His eyes darted sporadically around the yard and the house. That's when he saw it.

A small gate under the porch welcomed Adam's gaze.

He'd forgotten about that. Years ago, his dad used that five foot by five foot storage space under the porch for tools he generally used in the front yard. Adam never knew why his dad did that, but he was grateful for it now. Hopefully, the space wasn't jammed with unneeded tools; hopefully there was enough space for the bike.

Adam jogged the bike to the gate and lifted the latch. Since there were no hinges on the gate, he had to drop the bike in order to lift the gate up and over the closest bush. When the gate was far enough away, Adam scooted the bike into the opening. A few inches of clearance on either side of the bike relieved Adam.

Once the bike was in, Adam swiped the rocks together that had been separated from dragging the bike. He stood, replaced the gate and stepped back into the yard. He swung his vision over the landscaping at the front of the house and the porch. Nothing seemed out of place on first glance. The only way anyone—especially his father—would find the bike was if they walked up to the gate and opened it and looked inside.

Adam knew that was unlikely. His father mainly used tools from the shed now.

Good job, Adam. I'm glad you hid me under the porch. It would be a shame if your father found the bike, especially if it was in the front yard. No, under here is a good spot. Now that I'm taken care of, the blood is taken care of and your father is in the cellar with a strange bag, what are you going to do now?

"Go to my room," Adam replied to the bike.

Yes, you go to your room for being a bad boy. You've done lots of bad things today, haven't you?

Adam turned and went back inside.

In his room, Adam realized it was a matter of time before Victor's parents came looking for him and possibly sooner before they came calling or asking about their son. He was sure that Victor refrained from mentioning their adventure to his parents since they would probably forbid him from going. How would it sound if Victor said, *Mom and Dad, I'm going over to Adam's house to check out a creepy door his dad painted gold. We're going to go in there and see what's behind it and hopefully not be dismembered and eaten by a strange little plump monster hungry for little boys. Little boys who get curious and* need *to find out what's behind golden doors. Little boys who deserved much more than a good old-fashioned switching.* And Victor would say "switching" with the full pronunciation of "-ing" because that's how he was when he talked. The problem was that Victor would say all that other stuff. Adam was definitely sure Victor kept their little journey a secret from his parents.

Still, they would probably at least call. They'd ask for Adam and pose the questions, "When's the last time you saw him?" and "Did he come over this morning?"

and "Where do you think he went?" and "Do you think he's at the quarry again?" (Because the quarry was one of Victor's favorite places to go) and Adam might even suggest the warehouse just to give them someplace to look. He'd tell them they went there the other day and snuck inside just to see what it was like and he wanted to go back. Maybe he went by himself.

Adam nodded. That's what he'd say. Hide a lie with a truth. If his father taught him anything—besides how to whip a kid good with a nice stick—then it was how to hide a lie with a truth.

Okay, now that that problem was solved, he had to focus on what he would tell his dad if he figured out something went on in the hallway. *Hide a lie with a truth.* Of course that should be the plan. With his dad, though, he needed to be careful. What if he told a truth that would have consequences? Appease his dad in answering the issue of the hallway while appeasing the mean side. He was throwing a ball against the wall by his and Tommy's room and it bounced around the corner and hit the door. That could explain the few, small scratches left behind by Victor's foot. For disturbing the door, he'd get *switched* for sure, but that would be nothing compared to what would happen if his father found out what had actually happened.

That story hopefully wouldn't need to be spoken if his dad noticed nothing.

Adam forgot how long he stood outside his bedroom. However long was enough time for his dad to shut the cellar doors and enter the house through the kitchen door. Heavy boots stomped on the linoleum and paused. The refrigerator door broke the insulation, probably handing out a beer. *Here you go, Joe, for a good morning's work of laziness.* Maybe the garbage bag was full of money, pay for a good morning's work of something.

Laziness, Adam thought. For laziness, he knew whatever was in the bag was not money.

The fridge door sealed itself and the boots shuffled from the kitchen to the main hallway. His father's shadow rolled across the wall and led the way over the carpet.

Adam dashed back into his room, grabbing a book as he fell onto his bed.

"What's going on?" His brother asked.

With a finger to his lips, he *shhhh'd* Tommy and opened his book, Conrad's *Heart of Darkness,* to a random page. Luckily, he knew the book from cover to cover and only needed to read a sentence or two to recall what page he was looking at.

Their father trudged along, eventually making it up the stairs in tired movements. He passed their room, giving them a cursory glance and moving on. Adam kept his reading pretense as he shot a look at his dad over the top of the book. He hoped his father wanted to go to his room, which was right next door, and lie down—as the morning activities obviously made him exhausted.

Adam listened intently for the footsteps that would indicate his father entered his bedroom. It didn't happen. Instead, the booted footsteps continued, turning the corner, fading slightly since the sound had to go through two walls and various pieces of furniture.

Now, Adam never really paid attention to how many steps it took to walk from the corner of the hallway to his mother's bedroom—or more recently, the golden door. How many times had he walked that same length?

Weekly? Daily? Hourly? If he knew a day like today would come, he probably would have counted the steps and retained that information. He never had, but it didn't matter, a genius could figure out where his dad walked.

The footsteps stopped.

The silence became heavy, pushing down on Adam until he thought his heart was going to stop. He heard the soft *hwisssssh* from the hallway as he laid his book on the bed. Tommy's close-mouth breathing and the very light breeze rustling the leaves of the backyard oak tree joined the strange sound. Was there an airplane passing by overhead? He thought so.

Tommy looked up and said with his eyes, *What's going on?*

Adam pointed to the hallway, *Dad is at the door. He knows. He's got to know.* Adam didn't know if his brother understood what he meant by pointing to the hallway; he didn't know if Tommy really understood all the ramifications that would filter down to them if their father noticed one hair on the golden door's head out of place. *Be ready for the wrath,* the point also said.

"Boys," came their father's voice. It was calm and suspicious at the same time. Loving and mean. "Boys." Louder this time.

"Yeah, dad," Adam responded.

"Come into the hallway. Both of you."

Tommy's eyes told Adam he didn't want to, but Adam grabbed his brother's arm and pulled him off the bed. He whispered, "I don't think he saw anything."

They both went into the hallway, apprehensive. *No,* Adam thought, *not apprehensive. Something more, something beyond apprehensive. Simply not wanting to go into the hallway for the reason of not really wanting to was the right attitude.* They were scared. They feared what they might encounter in the hallway, with their dad waiting for them.

Adam saw a portion of their father around the corner. He hadn't really gotten as far down the hallway as he thought. He saw the untucked brown flannel shirt, the wrinkled khaki pants with strange dirt patterns on the thigh and the butt and the muddied heels of the boots. Adam noticed this mud in footstep clumps leading from the stairs to the spot their father now stood.

He turned when they were within a few feet. "Boys," he said, still calm. "Would you guys like to go to the movies?"

Adam and Tommy looked at each other, dismayed. This obvious movement made their dad smile. He *smiled.* "I know, I know. It hasn't been easy living with me. I just want to do something nice for you boys."

"I...I...guess?" Adam asked, or said. He couldn't tell if his own sentence was a statement, disbelief or a question.

"Are you sure, or not sure?"

"Sure," Tommy said. "I want to go see a movie."

"Great!" Their father reached into his pocket and removed a couple of bills. Adam saw a few twenties and some tens. He peeled of two twenties and handed them over.

Adam took them. "Are you coming?"

"No. Just you two. There's forty bucks there for movies and popcorn and then to get some lunch after."

"Okay, dad. Thanks." Adam stuffed the money into his pocket, skepticism still running rampant through his brain.

"And no rated R movie. Still gotta keep it clean." Their dad whisked them around and lightly pushed them to the stairs. "Now grab your coats and get moving. There's probably a few movies starting soon."

They got their coats—Tommy a windbreaker and Adam a hooded zipper coat—and found themselves standing on the front porch a minute later. Without turning around, they heard the door shut behind them.

And then the lock clicked.

With a low voice, Adam asked, "Tommy, isn't that strange?"

"A little. We should go to the movies."

Adam turned around and softly put his hand on the front doorknob. When he went to twist it, he found that it *had* been locked. Their father had *locked* them out.

CHAPTER NINE

That Afternoon

With forty dollars, they saw two movies and loaded up on popcorn and candy. They decided against lunch because the second movie started exactly ten minutes after the first one and the second movie was one they really wanted to see. All of their friends had seen *Iron Man 2* and Adam didn't think it would be in the theaters too much longer. The first movie had been about aliens from a distant planet invading Earth with the humans trying to survive the onslaught, but the twist was you learn about halfway through the movie that Earth wasn't being attacked, but that humans had occupied an alien planet years ago and the aliens were ousted, only to return 50 years later to reclaim what was once theirs. Adam thought it had good special effects and a weak storyline.

They still had about fifteen dollars left over—*Town Cinema's* concession pricing was lower than most, especially than the mall theater and the big 20-screen monstrosity over in Haleton. Four screens were plenty for this town and he and his brother had hit up half of them in an afternoon.

"Did you like *Iron Man*?" Adam asked Tommy.

"I did! Better than the first one."

"Yes it was."

Adam looked at a lamppost clock on the corner across the street. It read 4:35. "Are you ready to go home?"

"Yeah. I'm a little tired." Tommy did look tired, his eyelids ready to shut completely if he sat or lied down for five minutes.

"Maybe we should get some fast food for dinner. Dad would probably like that." Adam looked down the street and saw Burger King inviting him to spend the rest of the money. "How about Burger King?"

"I love Burger King." And Adam knew that, which is why he suggested it. *Paul's Diner* had good food as well, but they'd have to wait a little bit.

"Let's go get some burgers and head home."

Adam relished the walk home. Sure, he'd have to reheat the hamburgers in the microwave, but they would still taste fine. Maybe his dad would be grateful for his thoughtfulness. Tommy carried his own bag—Whopper Jr., small fries and a root beer—and walked with a pace that said *can't wait to get home and tear this bag open and tear into this food*. Adam held a larger bag with his Whopper and fries and his dad's two Whoppers and large fries. Actually, he could understand Tommy's rush to get home: the burger smell wafted to his nose, his stomach reminding him just how hungry he was. Well, he did miss lunch.

They arrived home a little after five. The front door remained locked, so they headed around the side of the house to go through the kitchen door.

When they turned the corner, Adam saw his father shutting the cellar doors. He turned the latch, securing the doors in case a strong wind visited the back yard; there had never been a lock on the door, just a latch with a hook and an eyelet. Their dad looked up.

"Hey! Back from the movies, eh?" He exclaimed, monotone.

Adam nodded. "We brought dinner."

"Burger King. Sounds wonderful." He waved a hand to the kitchen. "Let's go inside and eat."

Something was different with him again. This morning, niceness, and now suspicious indifference. Adam entered the kitchen, realizing that this Joe—his father—was a welcomed change from any of the Joes—his father—from any moment in time previous.

Inside, all three of them sat at the table, with Adam doling out the food to the proper family members. Without another word, or the usual "okay" from their father, everyone dug into their burgers.

The meal proceeded in the same silent manner because either the food was too good or no one really had anything to talk about. While they ate, Adam stole fleeting glances at his father—who concentrated harder than one should on the meal—to see if any telling signs about the hallway fell on his face. Through the entire twenty-five minute dinner, Adam found nothing that told him his father was suspicious and ready to command him to get a stick or a branch or worse, a baseball bat. A racing thought shot through his head: would his dad ever tell him to get one of Tommy's wooden bats? The thought quickly dissipated as his father wadded up his burger wrapper and tried to hook-shoot into the garbage. He missed by a foot and then laughed.

"That was a little off, huh?"

Tommy smiled and nodded. "The Bulls aren't going to call you anytime soon." That comment received a loving slap on the shoulder.

"Good one, son!" They both laughed.

"Nice one," Adam said.

"Adam, do you mind taking the garbage out? I know it's Tommy's night but I think me and him are going to watch some TV." His father turned to Tommy. "Would that be okay?"

"Sure, dad. Can we watch Disney?"

"You bet."

Adam agreed to take the garbage out. A quick glance to Tommy confirmed that even he didn't know what to think about their father's newfound friendliness towards them. *Is this a good thing?* Adam thought. He supposed that if his dad continued to act like this over a period of time, then it probably *was* a good thing. That was the Optimistic Adam, who truly wanted his dad to be like this from this moment on. *He was like this before, wasn't he?* Adam couldn't remember. Of course, the Skeptical Adam bet the Optimistic Adam if the friendliness would stop tonight. *Five bucks says he does.* Optimistic Adam placed that bet.

Tommy and their dad went into the living room and Adam soon heard the young actors of some Disney showing placing them in a funny predicament. Funny was a relative term when associated with Disney. Some of the shows weren't too bad, but those shows that catered to an even younger crowd relied on making fun of parents and loud bodily sounds to get a laugh. Okay, some of that was even funny.

Adam finished cleaning the table, not even complaining when he picked up his dad's missed shot. The garbage almost reached the top and if any more trash was added, the bag would be hard to get out since everything else would bulge against the sides. And his dad hated that. Well, maybe not the new Joe. He might be okay with it.

The bag slipped out easily and Adam tied it with the red band and then slung it over his shoulder. On the way to the trash can near the shed, he gave a peek to the cellar doors, trying to see if anything odd spoke to him. He'd only been in the cellar twice in his lifetime: his dad forbade him and Tommy to go into the cellar, much like he forbade them to go into that bedroom.

Except the cellar doors weren't painted gold. They were painted a dark gray and since they had been painted so long ago, chipping starting to occur. Another couple of summers and the cellar doors would need repainting.

The 30-gallon black trashcan loomed hazily as he approached it. Adam lifted the lid and went to drop the garbage bag into it. He stopped. The bag fell from his shoulder and *flumped* to the ground.

Sitting on the top of the rest of the garbage was a large, crumpled black bag. By itself, that wouldn't have been an abnormal thing, but Adam noticed splotches of red near the drawstring of the bag and small dots of red something along the lip of the trash can. He bent over, taking a couple of sniffs. Besides the expected garbage smell, a metallic odor drifted into his nose. It made the back of his throat close in protest and Adam jerked back up.

That's blood, Adam's mind told him.

"Can't be," he told it back.

Adam shifted the black garbage bag around, not really sure what he was looking for. As he lifted various layers of the waded up bag, some of the blood transferred from the plastic to his hand. He withdrew his hand immediately, watching the smear of blood soak into the miniscule cracks in his hand.

It is *blood, you know that right?* Something deeper within him asked him this and he answered without thinking, "Yes."

The blood was still warm and shined in the light of the bright three-quarters moon above. That meant it was fresh. How fresh Adam didn't know, but if he had to guess, he'd have to say as fresh as of this morning, when he saw his dad dragging the bag from the truck to the cellar.

The cellar!

He placed the garbage from the kitchen on top of the black bag and then wiped his hand in the grass. The blood transferred once more, ending in blurry strokes on the blades of grass. Adam walked towards the house, angling away from the cellar to get a better view of the living room.

By the time he saw the glow to the TV, Adam ended up on the opposite side of the yard, right against the fence. He still couldn't see his brother or his dad. Before he could go into the cellar, he needed to make sure he had ample time to get in there, check it out and then leave.

Adam went back inside and stood near the living room. The TV belted out cheesy lines and studio laughter loud enough so his entry remained silent. His father and Tommy sat next to each other on the couch, watching an episode of *The Suite Life of Zach and Cody*—which Adam actually liked—unaware of anything else.

Back outside, Adam ran to the shed. At first, the door wouldn't open and Adam thought it may have been locked, but the door was just stuck. He jabbed at the door until it popped open. Adam caught it just before it slammed all the way open just to make sure no noise brought out an Angry Joe.

His memory told him the flashlights hung on hooks to his right, next to the window. Working fast, Adam bolted in, made a right and caught a glimpse of a few cylindrical objects resting on the wall. He grabbed one and palmed it until he felt the raised button. After his thumb found the rubberized cover, he pushed it and a thick stream of light flew through the window.

"Shoot," he muttered. He whipped the flashlight away and cupped the lighted end. A twist thinned out the light. He must have the Mag-Lite.

Figuring he could find his way from the shed to the cellar, he flicked the flashlight off when he emerged from the shed. Adam carefully closed the door until it tapped the jamb. He didn't want any complications when he returned the flashlight.

The trip to the cellar took about ten seconds. He reached the cellar doors and turned the light back on and aimed the beam at the handles. The latch rose easily, as did both doors: he lightly laid each door against the ground. Adam paused, listening for any footsteps or sounds to indicate his father had heard him.

Let's get in there and see if we can find anything and get out of here. Five minutes. All you get is five minutes.

Five minutes might actually be too much time, but something told Adam not to make it any longer than that. The antics of Zach and Cody would probably end soon. He wished he had a watch to check. No going back into the house. No more stalling.

Go in already! Adam's head whipped around, looking for the source of the voice. He thought the voice sounded like Victor's but how could it be? *Quit being a chicken. Just get down there!*

Definitely Victor.

"Victor?"

Adam knew there'd be no answer, but he called out again, this time in a whisper. "Victor, are you there?"

His deceased friend didn't answer in reality or in Adam's mind.

"Quit being a chicken," Adam told himself.

The flashlight beam played on the walls of the stairs, showing Adam years of mold (*isn't that dangerous?*), families of spiders and accompanying spider-webs (*not so bad*) and dirt (*okay, I can do this.*) As Adam took the first few steps, he saw boot prints embedded in the dirt, disappearing inside the dark of the cellar.

Like Victor disappeared in the dark of the bedroom.

Stop it! Adam screamed at his mind. *Stop making me afraid!*

No can do Adam-boy, it answered. *You got things to do and see down here that a certain Joe—your wonderful and loving dad tonight—definitely doesn't want you to see. Most definitely doesn't want you to see. And so you know this and you don't really want to go down there so you are trying to stall. You're already in here now and I just want to make sure you realize that when bad things happen, they will haunt you. I will make sure they haunt you. Just as little reminders. That's all. Now get down there and quit being a chicken!*

Adam took the rest of the steps until the cold of the cement floor pushed its way through the soles of his shoes. He moved the light ahead and the cellar opened before him.

A few years ago, Adam had to do a report on their house and found out it had been built in the 1940's when residential structures were supported by thick columns of beams. Four such beams held up this house. For those wanting a complete basement they would be disappointed to find out the beams were decorative obstacles since there was no way to build symmetrical rooms. Things would just look odd and out of place. That was probably one of the reasons Adam's dad didn't make a basement family room. That and he needed the cellar for other tasks.

Besides the beams, nothing else sat in the cellar. At one time, Adam remembered this area held a washer and dryer, but his dad had created a utility room upstairs and moved both units there for convenience a few years ago. As Adam swept the light across the cellar, he saw the dust outline of where the washer and dryer used to be. The one little cellar window was caked with dust and filth and would take more than old-fashioned elbow grease to get cleaned.

The beam of light continued its travels and moved over something newer in the cellar. Something that looked like it didn't belong. Adam almost missed it.

He took a few steps towards the new find and as he got closer, he immediately knew what it was: blood. If he didn't know any better, Adam thought that someone had taken the dots of blood from the garbage bin and placed them down here in the cellar. One exception remained: more of the blood existed here than on the garbage can.

Adam counted seventeen little dots and kept moving in a line, still counting. When he got to thirty-five he stopped because now the blood looked up at him in clusters. Thicker and in more abundance. He stopped a foot from the wall opposite the cellar doors. The blood was in a circle, rising above the floor in a smooth bubble.

Looking up, Adam saw that he stood at the hole in the wall created for the newer pipes necessary to stay up to code. A water heater was also in there. Adam and Tommy had been here when they knocked out the wall and dug about ten feet into the ground. No cement in there; just a room of dirt.

Reluctantly—probably because Adam knew the outcome of his curiosity would not be good—he shone the flashlight into the hole. He placed a knee on the dirt ledge, expecting to go in a little further, but he saw all he needed to see.

Massive amounts of blood—more than Adam would ever have thought someone could hold in their body—pooled in different spots in the room. The puddles rested like syrup, undigested by the soil. His eyes moved towards the back of the dirt room and that's where he saw the decapitated head.

The source of the blood made sense now and the female head lolled at a slant, her eyes staring directly at him. Her long hair was matted to her head and her face contained dirt patches that almost looked drawn on by a make-up artist for her role as a homeless woman. Strings of neck muscles curled and hung loosely, as if the slice to the head had not been a clean one. *A saw?* Adam let out a tiny shriek and stumbled back in shock, dropping the flashlight. He fell backwards, catching himself with his hands, and landed on one of the larger masses of blood. The blood started seeping through his jeans, staining the fabric forever. Like the blood, he also would not be able to get the image of the head out of his mind forever.

He jumped up, hearing the sickening *swwaaaaf* as he realized his hands had also landed in a pool of blood. After quickly wiping them on the jeans—he may as well since he planned to throw them away—he picked up the flashlight with his shaking hands and made one quick sweep across the room with the light.

On a fast glance, everything seemed fine, except for the smeared blood on the floor. He didn't have time or the stomach to fix it and ran around the drops of blood to the stairs. Without knowing why, he turned back and aimed the light to the hole. He saw the upper right quadrant of the woman's head, the one eye saying to him, *It's not nice to leave chopped off heads all alone in a cellar. I need some company. Will you stay with me?*

Adam answered her by running up the stairs and closing the cellar doors.

As he entered the kitchen, Adam still heard Zack and Cody on the television. That meant it hadn't hit 8:30 yet, so at most he was in the cellar for twenty minutes.

Luckily, neither his dad nor Tommy would see him as he went from the kitchen to the hallway, up the stairs and to his room. Even so, Adam hurried: the blood on his pants would be extremely hard to explain.

In his room, Adam shut the door as quietly as he could, but forgot about holding the doorknob completely to the left or right: the door latch clicked loudly into the jamb plate. Adam was sure that was enough to bring his dad running with suspicion. After a few minutes of listening at the door, Adam became satisfied his dad didn't hear the click.

Within seconds, Adam stripped himself of the jeans, careful to keep them off the floor for fear of rubbing blood on the carpet. The blood may have dried by now, but he didn't want to take that chance.

He glanced around his room, wondering where he could hide the jeans. If he put them in the dresser, the jeans might taint his other clothes and his closet offered no convenient spot. Both his and Tommy's bed were raised high of the ground, so under them was no good. However, between the mattress and the boxspring might work. He walked over and lifted the corner of the mattress and stuffed in his jeans as far back as he could get them. At first, they bunched into one lump, but Adam got a better hold of the mattress and managed to smooth out the jeans.

Adam lowered the mattress and stepped back. No rise or separation occurred where the jeans were. That was good. His dad rarely came into the bedroom anyway, but why take that chance?

With the problem of the jeans solved, Adam found another pair similar to the blood-stained jeans. As he put them on, he saw a ghostly outline of the decapitated head in the mirror. This time, though, she was grinning. As she stared, flakes of skin slid off, exposing facial muscles and bone. Adam knew it was just in his mind, but it served to remind him he needed to do something about it. He witnessed Victor dying and now he saw a head in the cellar. He couldn't tell Tommy about the head; it was bad enough he had to see Victor die. Adam wondered how Tommy felt about their nice dad watching television with him.

Two things occurred to Adam at that moment. First, had Tommy spilled any information about what happened? Maybe all this niceness was a ploy to get a confession or admission of some sort from Tommy. Maybe his father *actually* knew something, but didn't have enough evidence and knew Adam wasn't going to say anything. So why not try for Tommy? Made sense; a little scare tactic might work on a nine-year-old.

The other thing that occurred to Adam was that his father didn't notice how long it took him to take the garbage out. Twenty minutes just seemed ridiculously long, especially for his dad, who probably was itching for a *switchin'*

Itchin' for a switchin'. His dad would love that. Maybe the next time it came for a *switchin'* he'd have to mention it; it might save his rear for once.

Still, he had been gone for twenty minutes. Was that enough to make his dad curious? Curious to what his oldest boy might be finding in the trash can, in the cellar? *Oh, you found something good, didn't you*, his mind said. *What are you going to do with that newfound knowledge?*

He had to do something, before he found anyone else.

Anyone else's head. Like his brother's.

Someone had to know.

CHAPTER TEN

The Next Morning

Once again, their father left and Adam and Tommy both watched him leave in the truck, heading in the same direction and last time.

"Again?" was all Tommy could say.

"I guess." Adam turned from the window. "I need to go somewhere also."

"Where?"

"I can't tell you. But you can't come with me."

"Why not?"

"Would you quit asking questions?" Adam snapped. Tommy's face dropped. "I'm sorry, Tommy, there's something I need to do alone."

That satisfied his brother, who grabbed a pair of pants, a T-shirt and baseball mitt and left the room.

"Tommy?" He called out.

Adam heard footsteps stop.

"You'll be okay for an hour by yourself?"

A few seconds of silence, then "Yes."

"And you won't go into the bedroom?"

Another few seconds of silence, then "I won't go."

"Do you promise?"

"Yes."

Tommy didn't *need* to go with him. Adam didn't want Tommy to hear what he had to say, to tell, to hear any words about the disasters of the past few days. Especially about what Adam found in the cellar. He didn't think his brother could handle it.

Slipping on a brown sweater and corduroy pants, Adam grabbed some change from his nightstand. Tommy stood in the bathroom grooming his hair. Adam was sure he saw him put a dab of mousse in his hand and run it through the top of his head. Adam laughed to himself.

On his way out the front door, Adam grabbed his windbreaker and headed to the gas station.

The two block walk to the gas station was into the wind. By the time Adam saw the Mobile sign— advertising 12-pack Cokes for 3.99 and 79 cent fountain drinks…Any Size!—his cheeks burned red from the stinging wind. Looking across the street at the bank's digital sign, Adam waited for the short pieces of information to flash by until he saw the temperature: 52 degrees.

That seemed awfully chilly for a summer day. Had he heard it would be cold today? He made a mental note to check the weather for the rest of the week when he got home.

A few cars sat at the gas pumps and another one filled a parking spot. The front of the station was a city of stacked pop cases and water and pallets of mulch. Signs littered the windows with cigarette advertisements and other monthly specials. The most important sign Adam was looking for was the small blue one with a phone symbol dangling from the overhang. Adam headed for the sign and soon saw the silver and black pay phone on the wall.

There were witty graffiti sayings etched and written on the metal coin box surrounding the phone. The phone book had long since been removed from the chain, but Adam found it tucked in the slot under the phone. He pulled it out and was relieved the front cover remained.

The inside of the front cover had the number he needed: the police. He found the non-emergency number and picked up the receiver. Adam dug out the change he took earlier and spilled it on the small ledge reserved for last minute scribbled numbers and other notes. He started to dial the number, but stopped. No dial tone. Adam tapped the tilting switch and waited for the dial tone, but all he heard were passing cars.

Grabbing his change, he committed the police number to memory and headed towards the entrance to the gas station.

The bell above the door dinged as Adam walked in and the middle-aged, unshaven clerk pulled his cigarette from his mouth and said, "Hello there, young man. Cold as a witch's tit out there ain't it?"

"I guess," Adam responded.

"You don't know what a witch's tit is, do you?"

Adam shrugged.

"No, I suppose you don't." He took a sip from a Styrofoam cup—Any Size!—and puffed a few seconds on the cigarette. "Well, what can I do for you?"

"Your pay phone's broken."

"Been broken for years. No sense it fixing it with those cell phones all about." The clerk waved his cigarette towards Adam. "Don't you got one of those cell phones? I see all kinds of kids your age talking on cell phones. Hell, some are talking when they aren't even talking; typing things on those impossibly-sized phones."

Adam could sense the man wanted to say "ain't." He could tell by the way he used the word "aren't"; a pause right before he said it, as if he was trying to impress a 14-year-old with his proper English except it sounded worse. The clerk should just say "ain't" because it would probably sound more natural.

"I don't have one," Adam said.

"Good, good. You don't need one. You don't want to be stuck years from now always on your phone, addicted to checking it every three minutes no matter where you are. I've seen people checking their damned phones in church. *In church!* Now if that ain't a sin, I don't know what is!"

That was a perfect ain't, Adam thought.

The more this man talked the more Adam's courage to make the phone call lessened. "Do you have another pay phone?" He asked.

"Sure do. In the back corner there." The clerk beckoned Adam to come closer. "Let me tell you a secret about that phone. Just between you and me."

Adam moved a few steps closer.

The man whispered, "Save your coins, young man. Just *fwapp* the phone on the side. Like this—" He slapped the air as if he were slapping someone's cheek. "You'll hear a click. The phone'll think you put in a quarter. Do that every time you need to. I ain't ever seen it not work."

"Thank you," Adam said.

"Now that's just between you and me. If you tell anyone, I'll have to have that phone fixed and I'll have to pay taxes on it." The clerk noticed someone coming up the far aisle, which held a number of coolers. "You all set?" The clerk asked the man.

Adam made his way down the middle aisle and found the phone in the corner. This pay phone looked exactly like the outside one except a little cleaner. He picked up the receiver and heard a dial tone. *Okay, step one complete.* Mimicking the action the clerk showed him, Adam slapped the side of the pay phone. At first, Adam thought he'd done it wrong since the dial tone continued its monotonous hum, but after a couple of seconds, the tone broke up into three short beeps before returning to a solid, annoying noise. He punched in the numbers from memory and heard each note push through the earpiece.

Three short rings later, a sharp female voice answered. "Hello. Seeton Police Department. How may I help you?"

"I need to report something."

"Okay, sir, what would you like to report?" It was funny hearing her call him sir.

"It has to be anonymous."

A short pause. "That's fine sir. What is the problem?"

"I saw a decapitated head." Adam didn't want to go into too much detail. His stomach started to knot and suddenly he just wanted to say it and get off the phone. "And a boy die." Did she understand him? How much did he really need to tell her?

"Sir, before you continue, I must inform you that prank calls are a serious offense that could get you up to 180 days in jail and a $500 fine. Do you wish to continue?"

"This is not a prank call."

"Is the place you saw the head and the boy the same place?"

"Yes."

"What is the address please?"

A hundred things flooded Adam's mind at that moment. What if their dad was caught? Where would he and Tommy go? Were they going to live somewhere else? An orphanage? Maybe with an older couple with other adopted kids who just wanted to milk the system for money? He's heard of that before. Would he and Tommy be able to remain together? If not, would they ever see each other again? Be allowed to keep in contact? Would they know anything about each other?

What if their dad wasn't caught? Would he find out who called? Would he assume that either he or Tommy tattled on him? Would the consequence be worse than any consequence ever? Adam figured he probably wouldn't be able to show his face in school: maybe not his face, but he couldn't go to school since he might not be able to sit down. Would they be able to live with their dad after that?

Adam realized that either way he looked at it, he and Tommy were leaving the household. He wished he knew at least one other family member, but he never heard their dad or their mother talk about relatives. Surely someone had to know who he's related to: a distant cousin or Aunt or Uncle he didn't know about. People had to know how to look that stuff up, right? Adam wasn't sure and hoped if the time came to it, he'd find the right person to help him.

"Sir? Are you still there?" A voice snapped him out of his worst-case scenario thoughts.

Hold on, hold on. Adam closed his eyes and took a deep breath. He couldn't be selfish right now. A decapitated head, Victor, Tommy: he had to think about now.

"Yes, I'm still here."

"The address please."

Adam game her the address.

"Can we please have your name?"

"No. I need this to be anonymous."

"What if we need to contact you for a statement?"

Adam hesitated, almost giving the woman his name. "I already gave you one. Goodbye."

He set the receiver back in the cradle and held this pose for a moment. *It's done,* the phone said to him. *You can't take any of it back. They probably recorded everything you said. They'll probably even figure out who you are, Adam.*

Turning away, he saw the clerk come out from behind the counter.

"You okay there, young man?"

Adam nodded.

"You don't look so good."

"I'm fine."

"Your face. It's a strange color, like you're sick or about to throw up or something."

The clerk was right, now that he mentioned it. A little butterfly was hitting the walls of his stomach trying to escape through his esophagus. Adam took a swallow and that seemed to work. The clerk walked over to a cooler and removed a bottle of pop and returned, holding it to Adam.

"Take this. It'll make you feel better."

It was a bottle of Sprite. Adam looked up at the man.

"It's okay," he said, "it's on me."

Adam took the bottle and twisted off the cap. The cold, carbonated liquid soothed his throat and landed in his stomach with a satisfying plop. "It's good," he told the clerk.

"Hope you feel better there, young man."

On the way out, Adam said, "Name's Adam."

The doorbell dinged and Adam made his way home.

CHAPTER ELEVEN

Two Hours Later

"So you're not going to tell me where you were?"
Tommy asked after Adam finished eating a sandwich.

"Nope. No need to."

"You were gone for two hours. I was bored!"

"When in doubt, read a book."

"I hate reading."

"Since when?" Adam picked a few crumbs off of
his shirt and flicked them to his bedroom floor.

"Since it's so close to school and I'll have to do it
so much there."

"That's not an excuse."

"I know. I'm just *sooo* bored."

"You're always so bored. Did dad come back at
all while I was gone?"

"No. Why?"

"No reason. Just wondering if he's going to leave
every morning for a few hours."

"Like you?"

Adam felt a flare of anger flow over his body, but Tommy couldn't be faulted for fearing Adam would turn into their father. He grabbed his brother and picked him up. "Oh yeah? Like me, huh?" Adam tossed him on the bed and started to tickle him. "Maybe I'll tickle you for a few hours."

Below them, a rough, deep knock erupted through the house. Adam and Tommy froze.

"Who's that?" Tommy asked.

"How would I know? I can't see through walls."

They left the bedroom and started down the stairs. From far into the house, they heard, "I'll get it!"

Adam looked at Tommy. "When did he get home?"

"I don't know. I didn't hear him."

"Did he come home while I was gone?"

"I don't know."

They saw their dad's shadow arrive before their dad actually did. He wore his boots and they pounded through the hall. Their dad stopped at the door and looked through the small, vertical window on the right. Why he did that, Adam didn't know: he never could see anything through the glazed glass.

The door opened and a thin man, taller than their dad by a few inches, stood on the porch. The man's black hair looked like it hadn't been combed or even washed in a few days and his clothes were well-worn. Adam recognized Victor's father.

"Hello," his dad said. "What can I do for you?"

The man's eyes drooped, sad. "I don't know if you remember me, we met only once before. I'm Victor's father, Mike."

"Hi Mike. I'm Joe," he said, offering his hand. Mike ignored it, but probably out of inattention and not rudeness. "What can I do for you?"

"I'm wondering if you've seen Victor. He hasn't been home in a couple of days. I thought he might be here."

Adam shot Tommy a fearful look, then pointed to the top of the stairs. They quietly sprinted to the landing, where they couldn't be seen, but could still hear what was going on.

"No," Joe said. "I haven't. I really haven't seen Victor in a few weeks, since my wife's funeral." Their dad said "wife's funeral" in a way that made it seem his family's death was much more important than Victor's disappearance.

"Has Adam seen him?"

"I don't know. Have you called the police?"

"Not yet. I wanted to make sure I checked all the possibilities."

"You should probably call the police."

"Yeah, I know." Mike lingered on the porch a little longer. He made a subtle movement to leave the porch, but stopped. "Is Adam home? I would like to ask him—"

"No. He's at the store."

Mike's dejection washed over his body. "Would you have him call me? I'm sure he has the number, but if he doesn't—" Mike removed a business card. "Here's my card with my home number on it."

Joe accepted the card with indifference and jammed it into his pocket without looking at it. "Sure. If I remember."

"If you want, I can call."

"I'll have him call," Joe said shortly.

"Okay. Thank you," Mike was saying as the door slowly closed on him.

When the front door clicked shut, their dad stood there, glaring at the possibility Mike remained on the other side. He turned. Adam and Tommy shot back out of sight. They heard those heavy boots across the floor again, entering the kitchen and exiting out the back door.

Adam dashed to the window. He watched his father head towards the cellar doors.

He's going to find out. He's going to go into the cellar and immediately know that I've been in there. And he's going to be mad.

"Tommy, stay in our room," he commanded.

"Why?"

"Don't ask, just do it."

Adam watched Tommy stare into his eyes and saw something serious in the command, something fearful.

"Okay," Tommy said, "I will."

When Tommy went into the bedroom, Adam went downstairs and sat in the living room. By the time he sat down on the couch, he heard the cellar doors slam shut. And not with a simple drop from a normal height, but with a slam that was created with a force of a hundred men dropping something from a hundred feet up.

He knows. He has to know. It's going to be a good switchin' time for him tonight. Why did I ever go in there? There couldn't be a reason I had to go in there. But I did.

The TV's screen reflected his slumped body back to him.

Well Adam, the TV said. *You're in it now, aren't*

you? It's only a matter of time before he figures out what happened in the bedroom. You'll probably tell him as he's beating you with a tree branch. And believe me, my young Adam, it will be with something other than a branch tonight. Yes, sir! Maybe one of those bats you thought of earlier or a two by four or maybe even his hands...that would be different, eh? Even if you don't tell him yourself he'll figure it out. When it comes to doing shady things, your dad takes the cake. He's not all up there in the book smart department, but when it comes to other things, he's got it made. You are just a peon in his world, Adam; you may as well know.

Footsteps halted near the living room.

"Adam," his father said. "Where's Tommy?"

"Upstairs."

"Good. I want to talk to you."

Adam turned, watching his TV self shift as well. His father came to an uncomfortable close spot next to Adam and sat down. Inches separated them. His father continued to stare straight ahead; Adam watched his father in the TV tube.

"I'm only going to ask you this once and I want the truth immediately," his father said, his voice low, serious. "Do you understand?"

"Yes."

"Did you go into the cellar at all in the past two days?"

The question hung in Adam's mind, pointing different-sized knifes at all sections of his brain. The question only pertained to the cellar and *not* the bedroom. Adam honestly didn't know which truthful answer was worse; he suspected both would cause him enough pain for weeks.

"Yes."

"When."

"Last night."

"Is that the only time?"

"Yes."

"Are you sure?"

"Yes."

His father turned to Adam, placing both hands on his knees. Adam watched the knuckles slowly turn white in the silence and then the fingertips a light red. The grip frightened Adam and he thought about jumping up and running out of the house, but it was already bad enough he admitted being in the cellar.

"*Why the hell were you in the cellar!*" His dad screamed. "*Who gave you permission to go into the cellar?*"

"No one."

"That's right no one! More importantly, *I* didn't give you permission!"

"I'm sorry, dad."

His dad shoved the apology away. "It's beyond the time for apologies." He used both hands to cup Adam's face and jerk it around so they were facing each other. "What did you see down there?" He growled.

A lie would be wrong. His dad was already angry and making him angrier while he held Adam's face may not be the best thing to do.

"Blood." Adam said, hoping that answer would satisfy.

It didn't. "Is that all? *Is that all?*"

"No. I saw a head."

"Yes. Yes you did, son." He grinned, his teeth taking on another presence in the mouth. Adam thought the teeth were going to jump out and take a bite off of his face. "That was Mary."

"Who was she?"

His father released Adam's chin and sat forward. "It doesn't matter. Go to your room, go do something just get away from me. I need to think. Things are not well for you."

Adam hesitated a second too long before standing.

"*Go!*" came his father's booming voice.

Adam ran up the stairs and into his room, shutting the door behind him. Tommy looked up from a comic book.

"What happened down there?" He asked.

"Nothing," Adam replied.

"That didn't sound like nothing. Why is dad angry?"

"He just is."

"Now he won't watch TV with me tonight, will he?"

Adam shook his head.

"I liked it when he watched TV with me last night. It's like we had a dad."

"I know, Tommy, but I may have made things unbearable for a while."

"How?"

"Not now. I want to rest."

Adam's eyes opened with him staring at the ceiling. He recalled lying down in his bed and Tommy leaving the bedroom. He also remembered his dad finding out about the cellar and questioning him about it. Surprisingly, he had answered truthfully, so that had to count for something, right? He didn't try to lie or pass off a partial truth as the entire truth. So while he didn't think he'd get off scot free, Adam knew that he did the right thing by admitting to his dad that he went into the cellar and found a head. Now that his father knows, maybe he'll stop doing whatever it is he's doing.

The clock on the nightstand read 2:47. A five-hour nap. He wondered what Tommy was up to. Adam spun out of the bed, putting his feet on the cold floor.

"Cold!" He walked to the window and saw the small temperature gauge mounted to the garage said 52 degrees. *Why is it so cold?* He asked himself and he couldn't answer the question. Adam shook his head as he grabbed a sweatshirt.

Then he saw Tommy standing in the middle of the yard, tossing a baseball into the air. More baseball. *Always baseball. At least he has something to take his mind off of everything. What do I have? More switchin'?*

Adam went downstairs and joined Tommy in the back yard.

"What are you doing Tommy?"

"Playing catch."

"Where's dad?"

"I don't know. He left. He looked mad."

"I'm sure he was."

"Wanna play catch?"

Adam shook his head. "No. I might go for a bike ride."

"In this weather?"

"Sure. It's not too bad. It's a damp cold, not a bitter cold."

"If you say so."

Adam walked over to the garage and wheeled out his bike into the grass. He checked the brakes and the chain. Everything seemed fine. He mounted the bike and gave it a heavy push on the pedals and he went forward a few feet. Perfect.

"Where are you going?" Tommy asked.

"Nowhere yet. Just checking my bike out."

"You always are. It will probably work for a thousand years."

"A thousand? Really?"

"Yep. A thousand." Tommy smiled and threw the ball in the air again.

While they stood in the yard, they heard the soft screeching of a braking car at the front of the house.

"Dad's not here?" Adam asked again.

"No. He left in the truck about an hour ago."

"I wonder who that is then."

Adam started walking towards the side of the house to get a peek of the car. He motioned for Tommy to follow and really didn't know if he would. As Adam crept along the side of the house, he saw the familiar stripes of the local police. Further movement revealed a big, gold POLICE decal on the doors. Red and blue lights, currently off, were mounted on top of the white car.

"It's the police," Tommy said.

"No kidding."

Of course Adam could guess why a police car sat in front of their house, but he still didn't feel like telling Tommy because a hundred questions would pour out of his brother's mouth. Not a hundred; probably a *thousand*.

Adam put his hand on Tommy's chest, stopping him.

The officer stopped halfway to the house, looking at the second floor. His right hand hovered over his gun while he said something into the microphone clipped to his left shoulder. The brown uniform with beige stripes fit tightly on the man though he appeared muscular. The strangest thing, Adam noticed, were the officer's shoes: white and red Nikes with Velcro strips. He didn't think they made shoes with Velcro on them anymore, but he supposed nothing ever really disappears.

The policeman found nothing of interest and continued up the porch steps. Adam and Tommy eased to the corner of the house to get a better view. When the man reached the door—hand over gun still—he knocked on the door four times. He turned and gazed out into the front yard. With no answer, he knocked on the door again seven more times. The officer stepped to the adjacent window and peered inside.

"What's he doing here?" Tommy whispered.

"I don't know. Why would I know?"

"Shouldn't we talk to him?"

Tommy was right. Adam found no reason *not* to talk to him. He was sure the officer was here to check out the claims of his anonymous call.

"Okay," Adam murmured, "Don't say a word about you know what. I'm going to talk to him."

"I won't."

As Adam and Tommy came around the corner, they heard the officer say "No one at the residence, base, coming—" Then he saw them and said, "Hold on."

"Hello," Adam called out.

The officer stepped back down the porch and met them halfway. "Hi there. Do you two live here?"

"Yes."

"I'm Officer James Harrington, but you can just call me James."

"Okay," Adam said.

"Where are your parents? I'd like to talk to them."

"Our mom died about a month ago and our dad is out."

"Sorry to hear about your mom." James finally moved his hand from the gun to his side. "Do you know when your dad will be back?"

"I don't know. Is there something we can do for you Officer James?"

"No, but could you give your dad something?"

"Sure," Adam said.

James reached into his breast pocket and took out a business card. "Give him this and tell him to call me as soon as possible."

"No problem."

"Hey! What's going on?" The voice came from behind the house. Adam peeked around the corner and saw his father storming towards them. "What are you doing? What are you asking them?"

James stiffened, returning his hand to the butt of the gun. "I thought no one was home. They came to me. I'm here to talk to you."

"What about?" Their father demanded.

"What is your name, sir."

"Joe."

"Last name?"

"It's not needed until you tell me what you are doing here."

Adam and Tommy silently made their way to the bottom of the porch steps. Adam badly needed to get away from this interaction. On the porch would be better. Scooting Tommy before him, he guided his brother to the top of the steps.

"I'm investigating an anonymous call," James said as he darted his eyes around him.

"An anonymous call? About what?" Their dad laughed. "What could possibly drive you down here?"

"We have received a report about your cellar, sir. Would you mind if I took a look?"

Joe nodded. "I would mind very much." Adam saw him shoot a glance towards the porch. He was sure the look was for him. "You have no cause to ask that."

"Actually, sir, the cause is a call."

"A prank call, no doubt."

"It's still something we have to look into."

"My answer is still no."

A static cackle flew out from James' microphone. He pressed the button. "Officer Harrington here."

A click, then from the mic, "You're needed over at Paulie's. Fight in progress."

James checked his watch. "A little early for that," he mumbled. He returned his look to Joe. "Since you haven't complied, then I must warn you if there is another call or complaint about this house, then a warrant will probably be issued."

"Fine," their dad said defiantly. "A warrant then."

James clicked the mic again. "Officer Harrington here. On my way to Paulie's."

Some other words came through as James headed back to his car, but they were garbled. Adam tucked the business card in his front pocket and watched his father glare at the police officer until the squad car sped away. The car's red and blue lights spun and when the car turned the block, its siren pierced the sky.

Adam whispered to Tommy, "Go inside and hide somewhere."

"Why?"

"Just do it," Adam whispered, sterner this time.

Tommy disappeared into the house through the front door.

"So," Adam's dad said. "What do you think is the reason for that cop to visit this house? This particular house on this particular day only a short time after you admitted going into the cellar."

"I don't know, dad," Adam said.

"I do," he said. "*And I don't like the answer!*" His dad stepped back and swiped his hand towards the backyard. "Get down here and let's go to the backyard!"

Solemnly, Adam trudged down the steps and hesitantly passed his dad. When his dad raised his hand to point to the backyard—as if Adam could forget how to get to the backyard and the reason for going there—Adam flinched, bringing both hands to his face.

"Ha!" His dad laughed hysterically. "Why would I beat you? It's more fun to *switch* you!"

Adam quickened his pace to the rear of the house. His father, too excited for the moment, rushed past Adam and stood in the center of the yard.

"Which one are you going to pick tonight?" His dad asked. "Is it going to be—" He pointed to a branch. "This one?" He pointed to another. "Or this one?" And another. "Maybe it's going to be this beauty!" Another. "I know: you got your eyes on this one!"

When Adam made no move to select a branch, his father walked over to him. "No way, right? None of those are good enough for you. I can see it in your posture." He shook his head. "No, no, no. A tree branch just won't do."

His father started towards the shed. "You know what? I got a special *switchin'* stick saved up for just an occasion like this."

Adam felt like running. He knew he could outrun his father easily, but that would leave Tommy to defend himself and who knew what his father would do to his brother. In a few days, if Adam visited the cellar again, it's very possible Tommy's head would be down there to join the woman.

His dad entered the shed.

Adam thought he had enough time to run into the house, grab Tommy and *then* run. Both of them could outrun their dad. They were healthy kids: Tommy played baseball and Adam liked to swim and ride his bike. Their dad was just a slob with a growing beer belly and a bad heart. The most exercise he probably got was decapitating heads.

With a shake of the head, Adam jiggled the thought out. No, running was out of the question.

What about fighting?

Adam's eyes scrunched. His mind was crazy. Fighting seemed more out of the question than running. Healthy did not mean strong. However, working at the mill at least gave his dad some meat on his arms and legs. No, Adam would be easily overpowered in seconds.

How about finding a quick weapon?

"Shut up," he told his mind. That idea made sense but wasn't practical. Where would he get a weapon in less than ten seconds?

His dad emerged from the shed, holding his *switchin'* stick.

More of a dowel, the pale wood was at least three feet long and about three inches in diameter. Adam knew that this stick was meant for hurting. No tree naturally made this piece of wood. His dad really meant it when he said it was a special one for just an occasion like this.

A quick glance to his bedroom window revealed Tommy staring down at the scene about to happen before him. Adam turned back towards his dad. If he was going to be hit as he thought he might, Adam vowed to scream as loud as he could. Surely someone would hear him.

Adam started to lower his jeans.

"No," his dad said. "Not out here. Do you think I'm stupid? This time's going to hurt." He pointed to the cellar. "In there."

"No, not in there."

The stick rose towards the sky. "Get in there or the first whack will be on your face."

Would anyone hear the screams in the cellar? Tommy probably would.

Adam lifted the cellar doors, apprehensive about lowering himself into the darkness without his flashlight. "I can't see," Adam said.

"Bullshit you shitbird." His dad gave Adam a little shove. "Use your memory from the other night."

Each step echoed in Adam's mind. *Thump. Thump. Thump. Thump. Thump.* Five steps. Both feet landed solidly on the cellar floor. Adam remembered the beams and walked to the middle of the cellar. He turned and saw his dad in the light from outside, which basically turned him into a black shadow with a stick shadow protruding from his hand.

"Are you going to kill me?" Adam decided to ask.

"Kill you? That would be stupid. This is just your normal, run of the mill punishment for calling the cops."

"I didn't."

"Hmm…for some reason, I don't believe you."

"I've been home all day. Ask Tommy."

Adam heard a slow chuckle coming towards him. "Right. You probably got Tommy all convinced to be on your side."

"I didn't call!" Adam yelled.

His dad ignored him. "Pants down."

"No."

"Do you want me to help you?"

"No," Adam said, defeated. He undid the button and lowered the zipper. Slowly, his pants drifted to the floor.

"Good," his dad said. "Now lie down, face on the floor."

Adam did as he was told. *This one's going to hurt, Adam. This one's going to be the switchin' of the century!* Adam closed his mind to the obvious and closed his eyes, hoping the pain would not exist.

Unfortunately, it did.

Adam tuned out his father's grunts and the excitement in his voice each time the dowel connected with bare skin. *Spare the child, spoil the rod. Is that how it goes? Spoil the child, spare the rod?* He didn't know. It was hard to concentrate, knowing an excruciating pain would follow a rushed *whoooooooosh* as the stick flew through the air. All he knew was the rod was doing a great job of *switchin'*.

Whaaaaaaack!

He could feel the welts rising immediately with each strike. Thighs, calves, butt: it seemed no part of his lower body was immune. Adam would have to remember to apply some salve later.

The count reached twelve and Adam's muscles were becoming numb. He tried to tense his leg muscles but it felt like he had been riding his bike for days anyway.

Thirteen, fourteen, fifteen, sixteen. *Is this going to end soon?* Adam asked himself. Seventeen, eighteen, nineteen, twenty.

Adam looked up and saw the decapitated head staring back at him. *A better question, Adam, is how could your dad still be going? Does he like it that much? I know he probably liked it when he cut my head off. Hey, I just got a great idea! He should do the same to you and then we can be Dirt Buddies! Wouldn't that be fun?*

But the head wasn't there. Adam closed his eyes and reopened them quickly. The vision was just a ghost in Adam's mind, something to focus on while his dad did his thing. Now that he was attentive, he saw the head was missing and tilting his head for a quick glance around the cellar, he also saw the blood wiped clean from the floor.

Your dad did a bang-up job of cleaning this place, huh? The head again. *Don't worry, though, I'll still be your Dirt Buddy.*

The distraction made Adam miss a few strokes. Twenty-five? Twenty-six?

There was a pause, but Adam was afraid to turn his head and see what was going on. His father's labored breathing pushed out in short bursts for a few minutes and then stopped. His dad was going for another one.

The *whooooosh* came down and smacked right into Adam's lower back. Something popped horribly and he hoped it was a muscle and not bone.

"Aaaaaah!" Adam screamed.

"Shut up. It wasn't that bad."

"You hit my back!"

"You're lucky that was the last one," his father grunted.

Tears fell to the floor, creating a tiny dark circle on the cement. Adam watched it expand outward, trying to let the initial pain of that last hit go away.

His dad tossed the rod near the entrance to the dirt hole. "My oh my," he said. "That was definitely a good stick. Have to remember to use that one again."

His dad's heavy footsteps reverberated against the foundation as he left the cellar. If there was one bright side to being left down here with the head, the musty odor and curious spiders, it's that his dad left the cellar doors open.

Adam thought about trying to get up, but everything about him was weak. His legs, arms, feet, knees, hands, and even his fingers suddenly became extremely lazy. Besides the physical toll he emanated, his will also gave up. He laid there for a few minutes before shutting his eyes, sleep quickly overtaking him.

CHAPTER TWELVE

Sometime Around Midnight

Adam's eyelids slowly parted, looking into an uncomfortable darkness. His stomach curdled and his mind tried to remember where he was exactly and why he seemed to be lying down.

Then, as if to answer its own question, his mind flashed a few scenes to help him remember. The decapitated head, his grinning father, the cellar doors, his walk inside, the thick rod pounding his body, the last hit on his back.

His back.

As soon as he remembered the final hit, Adam's back flared with uncontrollable pain. He grimaced and tried to twist the pulses away, but they were too strong. It was hard to tell if a bone had broken or if a muscle had been bruised. Arching his bad proved difficult and shot more pain through his body. He attempted to push up and he managed to prop himself on his knees like one of those Yoga positions. Good. A first step. He brought one leg forward and planted a foot on the floor. When he put some weight on the leg, his back screamed in protest, the joint near the top of the butt giving out. Adam fell to the floor, returning to his stomach.

He now faced a different way, towards the entrance. Nighttime floated its way inside, the moonlight illuminating most of the first half of the cellar. How long had he been sleeping here?

A shadow fell across the cellar door, slightly blocking the light. It paused for a moment before stepping down. It bounced with awkwardness and held something.

"Adam," the shadow said.

Tommy.

Adam watched his brother cautiously make his way to where he lay.

"Adam, are you okay?" he asked.

"Yes," said Adam feebly.

"I don't believe you." Tommy sat down near Adam's head. "I brought you something to eat and drink."

"Thanks."

"Can you sit up?"

"No. My back hurts a little."

"Can you move?"

"A little."

Tommy set down the plate of food and a can of pop and slid both hands underneath Adam's back. Without warning, his brother lifted. Adam's lower back shouted in pain again.

"Owww!" Adam yelped.

"I'm sorry."

"It's okay. Not your fault." Adam ignored the pain and sat all the way up. "Help me over to one of those beams."

Tommy curled his arms under Adam's armpits and pulled as Adam scooted. In five jerks, Adam was able to lean against the plastered support. He drew his knees to his chest; the back pain subsided slightly.

"Here," Tommy said, handing him the plate.

Adam took a bite of the sandwich. "Bologna and cheese. It's good."

"And a pop."

Adam lifted the tab and heard the comforting fizz greet him. He took a sip, enjoying the moment in the cellar with just his brother. Sure, his dad had just beaten his legs and back, but now Tommy sat next to him with comfort.

"We need to tell that cop," Tommy blurted.

Adam's bite of sandwich almost fell out. Something occurred to Adam in that voice. He couldn't place his finger on it, but it sounded determined, confident and extremely mature. Was his brother nine-years-old anymore? It sounded like it was going to *tell that cop* no matter what Adam or anyone else said about it.

"You still have his card thing?" Tommy asked.

Reaching down, Adam wiggled his pants up so he could get his hand in the pocket. Finally, he found the card in the left pocket. "Yeah, right here," he said.

"Let's call him tomorrow," urged Tommy.

"No, not yet. We need to get some proof."

"How?"

"I'm not sure right now. I need to get to my room first."

"Do you need help?"

Adam used the beam for support as he pushed against it and slid upwards. This wasn't so bad, actually. He managed to go completely upright. Now he had to try and take a step. He forced his right leg forward and it went. When the foot landed on the floor, a small area on his lower back tingled. The pain was trying to send him to the ground again. But he bore down and put a little more weight on the foot: his body held.

"I think I can make it," Adam said. "I might need help at the stairs."

Sluggishly, Adam took each step carefully. After a few minutes, he found himself looser than before and eventually made it to the cellar stairs with slight ease.

Five steps, Adam, you can do this.

It was like learning to climb the stairs for the first time. A foot goes on first, then the other foot goes on the same step. Repeat the procedure until the outside is directly in front of you. The night air was steeped in a thick fog. At least it had warmed up a little.

"What time is it?" Adam asked Tommy.

"Around midnight or so."

Adam made it to the kitchen door without incident and even through the kitchen—though he did think at one moment he might slip on the rug in front of the sink—and to the bottom of the stairs to the second floor. This obstacle loomed before him like an exaggerated monster for a children's story. Something he must slay.

But that too was conquered—but not in any record time—and soon, Adam walked across his bedroom floor and lowered himself into his bed. 1:13 a.m. his clock read.

What a ridiculous night, Adam thought. He patted the business card in his pocket. The cop needed to be called—Tommy was right about that one—except Adam wanted irrefutable proof that his dad was involved in something heinous—

That's the word: HEINOUS. He wondered if the cop would love to hear that word. That word would probably make Officer James Harrington and multitudes of backup come running. And the next time, his dad won't have any excuse or reason to deny Officer Harington admittance to the house or cellar.

He heard Tommy flop into bed.

"Tommy," Adam said.

"Yeah?"

"Thank you."

"Sure. Couldn't leave you down there all alone with the spiders. You might make a new friend and leave me behind."

Adam was positive Tommy had matured greatly in the last two hours.

"Good night," Adam said.

"Night."

CHAPTER THIRTEEN

Two Days Later

Adam didn't call the cop, nor did he or his brother get any proof. His back still hurt and he felt it necessary to remain in bed until he could walk smoothly. Couldn't let his dad see the weakness; he'd use it somehow.

So over the next two days, Adam remained confined to the bedroom, only leaving to go to the bathroom or find a book to read on the shelves in the living room—and he only went there when he knew his dad was gone. He read a Dickens' novel, a couple by Hemingway novels and a short story collection by Stephen King, which was the favorite of everything he read in that span.

Tommy continued to bug him about calling the cop, but after the first morning of the night after the excessive *switchin'* Adam angrily convinced his brother the logic of waiting for proof.

We have to make sure, he told Tommy. *We can't risk coincidence,* he said. *We have to make sure we don't see our dad after we tell.* It took a lot of statements like that to get Tommy to realize that dad was a dangerous man who was probably capable of hurting his kids way worse than a simple *switchin'*

I know, Tommy said. *I just want things to be over.*

I do too, Adam said, *but we should be smart about it.*

Tommy didn't bother him again with his pleading.

Their dad was gone most of the time. Adam only saw him once as he passed by the bedroom to check on the golden door. Once it opened, Adam listened for anything else, but only heard the door open and shut again, about thirty seconds later. Otherwise, their dad ate dinner alone, not complaining once he had to fix his own frozen dinners.

A bright spot was a call from Violet the second afternoon after the cellar incident.

"Hello," Adam had said.

"Hi. It's Violet."

"Oh, hi. How are you?"

"Good. How have you been? I haven't heard from you since the quarry."

"Been busy."

"Doing what?" she said.

"Watching my brother."

"That's a lot of watching." She sounded irritated, almost angry.

"My dad's been out of town."

"Has he?"

"Yeah. Helping his sister." Adam didn't even know if his dad has a sister, but at least the lie came out convincing.

"Is that why you haven't come over?"

"I didn't know you really wanted me to."

"Don't be stupid, Adam." She said his name forcefully, maybe to remind him she was in charge a little. *Just like a girl,* he had thought.

"Sorry. Just had things to do, that's all."

She paused. "Listen Adam, I like you. I want you to know that before school starts. I don't want us to get lost in the sea of high-schoolers and forget that we both existed. The next few years will be important for us. I don't know if that will mean together, but I just wanted you know that I like you."

Adam had smiled. He really didn't know what she was talking about. The only thing that made sense in what she said was that she liked him. The rest? Well, that was for philosophers to answer.

"Adam?"

"I like you too," he had said. He heard his father coming down the stairs and added, "I have to go. Talk to you later."

He quickly sat on the couch, flipping through a magazine as his dad walked by and out the door.

As he rested in bed that day and the next morning, he thought back to the conversation. Did he like her? Or did he just say it because she said it? He wasn't sure and after he found the proof he needed from his father, he'd have to figure out this whole Violet thing.

But first he needed a plan to get proof and he knew just how to do it.

CHAPTER FOURTEEN

The Next Day

Adam's back felt a little better, even though if he moved a certain way, small pokes of tenderness gave him tingles. He sat in bed, fighting the initial stiff pain and reached over on the nightstand for some aspirin and the glass of water. Tommy had been keeping the nightstand ready with pills and water at all times in case Adam needed them; he was extremely grateful.

With the tablets gone and the glass of water emptied, Adam slowly changed into a new set of clothes. When he put on his jeans, he tightened the belt as far as he could take it since the pressure relieved his back some as he walked.

Where was Tommy?

Normally, Tommy would be up and bugging him to do something: play outside, play catch, or he'd be begging to go somewhere. Adam looked at the clock. It was nearly noon; maybe Tommy was eating lunch.

Adam took a few steps to test his strength and deemed it okay to go down the stairs without assistance. When he reached the bottom, he called out, "Tommy?"

No answer. Adam went into the kitchen and saw two Lunchable packages on the counter. *He was eating lunch, but with who?* Surely their father didn't eat lunch with Tommy.

"Tommy?" He tried again.

He didn't hear any response from Tommy, but he did hear something bang below him.

The cellar.

Adam made his way outside and to the cellar doors, which were propped open. Voices filtered up through the stairs, causing him to step back. Who's down there? Adam cautiously took one step at a time. Images of his dad with that dowel rod flooded back to him.

In the cellar were his dad and Tommy. At some point, their dad had taken one of the lamps from the living room and placed in on the floor. Adam didn't even know there was an outlet in here. Although mostly focused to one side of the cellar, the light gave enough visibility to see that they had been cleaning up down here.

Busy little bees, came the voice of the decapitated head.

Adam glanced to the dirt room; Tommy stood only a few feet in front of it. The head was not there. It had been removed.

His dad stopped sweeping. "What do you want?"

"Came to see what the noise was," Adam said. "What are you doing down here?"

"We're cleaning!" Tommy answered.

"Yeah, we're cleaning," his dad said. "Is there a problem with that?"

"Why are you cleaning?"

A shrug. "It's dirty down here. Thought maybe we could do something with this place. Make it a *fun room.*"

Fun room came out as a gurgle, as if a deep laugh would soon follow. His dad smiled and returned to sweeping an already clean floor. Tommy had a mop and dipped it in a bucket of soapy water when Adam approached him.

"Hey Tommy."

Tommy plopped the mop on the floor, water splashing everywhere.

"You should kind of wring it out first," Adam offered.

His dad scoffed. "He's been doing fine. Leave him be."

Adam glared at his dad and then put a hand on his brother's shoulder and guided him towards the cellar doors. "Leave the mop, Tommy, I need to talk to dad."

Tommy squinted his eyes slightly, unsure if he should really leave the cellar. Adam nodded. *It's okay,* the nod told Tommy, who handed over the mop.

As Tommy walked away, their father said, "Oh, you have to talk to me, huh?" He leaned the broom against one of the beams. "Okay, what do you *need* to talk to me about?"

"Mom."

That one word made his dad frown. He was already frowning, but when Adam said *Mom* the frown turned from miserable to intense, ready to jump off his face and strangle Adam. First of all, his father probably didn't expect Adam to come down here; second of all, he probably didn't expect Adam to express a need to talk to him. Don't anger an already angry lion, Adam had heard many times. But then to mention his mother? His dad surely didn't expect that.

"What about that whore?"

Adam shot his eyes around looking for the rod his dad used the other night. It sat against the wall behind his father. In the light it didn't appear so menacing.

"Why did you treat her like you did?" Adam asked. As much as he wanted to scream, he wanted to keep his composure. He didn't want his dad steaming mad just yet.

"I don't know what you're talking about."

"You beat her," Adam threw out.

His dad laughed. "Beat her? How do you suppose?"

"I saw the bruises and the cut on her shoulder."

His dad locked eyes with Adam, who knew he'd search out a bluff at some point. *Keep your eyes on his,* Adam thought. *Don't look away. Once you do, he's got you.*

"Bruises and cut?" His dad took a step towards Adam.

Perfect. Adam matched the movement with one of his own, getting closer to the *swtichin'* stick.

Adam nodded. "You probably weren't aware that I went into mom's room on the last day she was alive."

"What?" The disbelief flowed from his eyes.

"You were drunk, passed out. *She asked for me, dad.* She asked for me on her dying day and you didn't even tell me." Adam continued to follow the stutter steps of his father. About thirty more feet now. "She gave

140

Tommy a note for me because she didn't trust you to tell me."

Adam could see anger starting to boil within his father, but he caught himself and smiled. *The words are right,* Adam thought. *The delivery isn't.* He had to think of a different and faster way to get him mad.

"You think you know it all, don't you Adam."

Hearing his name from his dad threw him off. When was the last time he heard his name uttered from those lips? His dad appeared suddenly calm.

"You think you have *all* the information," he continued.

"She told me *all* the information I needed that day. Did you regularly beat her? Did you think she was a target of one of your hammers? You got to pound her until she gave in?" Adam hoped that would spark something.

"Of course I thought she's something I could hit," his dad said sarcastically. "*That why I married her,* you stupid little shitbird." He managed to move in a couple more steps without Adam noticing. When he did notice, Adam jumped further away.

"Is that what she told you?" His father asked.

"She told me everything. You treated her like *shit!*"

"What did you say?"

"You. Treated. Her. Like. Shit." He repeated, emphasizing *shit.*

Another few steps in an arc found Adam about fifteen feet away from the rod.

"So that's what she told you?" His father asked. "It doesn't surprise me. She wanted to turn you and Tommy against me."

Adam paused in his journey across the cellar. "I don't believe you. I don't believe you at all. She just wanted to protect us."

"Who do you think put those bruises and that gash on your mother? Your mother did. Your precious, beloved mother. She did it with her favorite cutting knife. As a matter of fact, I think it's the same one you used to cut the chicken for your shitty casserole you made last week. Had blood on it at one point. Possibly blood from that gash you saw."

A mind game. That's all this was. His dad was playing a mind game with him. Trying to get into his head with lies. Of course he didn't believe his father. Why would his mother do those things to herself? It didn't make sense.

To turn you against your dad, his mind answered. *He just said that.*

Lies.

"Now are you wondering why she wanted you against me?" His dad asked.

"Well, if you are going to continue this lie, dad, I may as well hear the reason."

"Because she wanted me to hate you."

"You *do* hate us."

"No, I don't *hate* you. I find you and Tommy annoying as shitbirds, but I don't hate you."

"Then why do you *switch* us?!"

His father shook his head. "You may not understand now, but when you have kids of your own you will." He took two steps closer and Adam took two steps to the back and side. About ten feet now. "It's just my method of discipline, that's all. My father did it to me when I misbehaved and his father did it to him when he misbehaved."

"We don't misbehave," Adam countered. "You do it just to be a jerk."

"That's what I thought when my dad *switched* me, so it doesn't come as a surprise you'd say that."

"Did you *switch* mom?" Adam asked, spouting the question quickly.

"We're done talking about your mom," his dad said. "In fact, I'm going to ask a question now and neither one of us is leaving without an answer."

His dad stopped moving in Adam's direction and maneuvered in front of the cellar's entrance. This was a lucky break. Adam moved behind a beam and within a few feet of the thick rod.

"Have you ever gone into the bedroom after your mother passed away?" His dad asked.

"No," Adam said. It was the truth as far as the question was concerned.

"Has anyone else gone in the room?"

Adam paused a second too long.

"Like Victor for instance," his dad said.

"No."

"Now who's telling lies?"

"I'm not."

"Someone knows the truth and it's not me."

"What do you mean by that?"

His dad laughed. "So where is Victor? Have you seen him lately?"

"Sure a few days ago."

"Since then. I mean he *is* your best friend and all."

"No."

"Did you know his dad came to visit me? He thought Victor came here. Now why would he think that? Because you're his best friend?" His dad's voice became darker, threatening. "Some best friend you are, Adam, letting him die like that."

Adam had enough. He decided to ask the one question that would probably send his plan in motion. "So dad, what's in the bedroom? That thing? Where did you find it?"

"So you *do* know. You *have* been in there."

"I haven't been in there."

"But you've seen it."

Adam didn't answer. He took one giant hop towards the stick and grabbed it. Holding it out from his body like a sword, he aimed it at his father.

"What are you going to do with that," his father said, mocking. "You going to hurt someone with that?"

Adam shook it once, walking towards his father.

"You're liable to hurt yourself."

Adam started walking towards his dad. The only thing that would ruin the plan was if his dad decided to leave the cellar. Adam didn't think their positions would be like this and if he thought they would, Adam would have put himself between the cellar entrance and his dad. Unfortunately, there were too many factors going into the cellar than Adam could account for. He just had to hope his father didn't turn and exit. Of course, his father couldn't let a little annoying *shitbird* get the best of him.

"Such a stupid little shitbird you are," his father said.

A second later, Adam saw his father leap into a full sprint. He was not running to the entrance, but towards Adam.

With instinctive reflexes, Adam cocked the stick back as if he was going to use it as a sledgehammer and swung it horizontally through the air. His dad was moving too fast to move completely out of the way and took a solid hit on his bicep. He yelped and grabbed that arm. The force of the blow pushed his dad into the wall and bounced Adam backwards a few feet. Still erect, Adam's father tried again, this time slower and with both eyes on the stick. Adam held the stick in front of him again and poked it, stopping his dad cold.

"Think you're clever?" His dad mumbled as he strafed Adam.

Adam kept his dad in his sights by using the end of the rod as a point of reference. He poked, attempting to move his father deeper into the cellar, possibly near the dirt room.

"I'll show you clever."

His dad came again and when Adam tried his poking trick again, his dad sidestepped the rod and grabbed it inches from Adam's hands. When he pulled, Adam gripped harder and tugged. He knew he wouldn't be able to keep this type of strength up against his father for too long, so he tipped the scales to his advantage.

Adam launched a kick into his dad's groin.

A rough *uuumph* came from his dad's mouth and Adam found himself wheeling backwards since his dad's grip suddenly released. Adam caught his balance and came forward, his weapon poised to the side. Between tugging on the stick and kicking his father, his back started to throb.

His dad knelt on the floor, holding his groin and moaning. A stream of puke ejected to the floor, the putrid smell hitting Adam. The yellow, chunky eject dripped from his dad's mouth. He looked up as Adam stood over him about a foot back. With a loud grunt, Adam swung the rod downwards. A good portion of the stick, the last six inches or so, connected sharply with his dad's cheek.

A glob of blood—and Adam swore he saw a tooth—flew to the side and landed in the puddle of puke. His dad fell over, his eyes slightly rolling up into his head.

"Dad?" Adam said. "Dad?"

There was no answer.

Adam poked his dad in the stomach with the stick and received no movement in return. He knelt down and felt the chest. It rose and fell with a creepy calmness, but he wasn't dead. Just unconscious.

Before he left the cellar, Adam tossed the rod into the dirt room. He gave one more glance at his father and headed outside.

CHAPTER FIFTEEN

A Few Hours Later

Adam decided to visit Violet.

There was just one reason to visit Violet. She seemed to have a genuine interest in him and he wanted the friendship. He didn't know if it would go further than just a friendship, but something in the last day made him not afraid to find out. Actually, he knew what that something was. A little more confidence; a little more *bravado*.

Plus, he needed to borrow something from her, if she had one, and Adam hoped she did. Besides, why wouldn't she? Everyone seemed to have one except him.

The trip from Adam's house to Violet's took about fifteen minutes by bike. The air had warmed up a little in the middle of the afternoon but there was still something chilly as he pedaled through the neighborhoods.

He saw Violet's house—a simple ranch with a two-car garage—as he turned the corner. To Adam's luck, he also saw Violet outside, sitting on the porch steps reading a book. He was glad for that; an encounter with her parents might take some time and he didn't want to waste any.

Adam popped his bike over the curve, hopped off and walked up the path.

Violet looked up, smiled and wave, setting her book down on the steps. She slid a lock of her hair behind her ear and stood up.

"Hi!" She said.

"Hey, Violet."

"Come for that bike ride?"

Adam had forgotten about her request the day at the pool. *A bike ride. What would she expect? I rode a bike over here.*

"No, sorry, just came to say a little hello."

Violet's face dropped, disappointment flooding her eyes. "Just a hello? Okay."

Adam eyed the book, trying to keep the talk going while not becoming nervous. "What are you reading?"

"*Moby Dick.*"

That perked Adam. "Really? It's one of my favorites."

"For me, not so much. My mom said I should read it since I'll probably end up reading it for school anyway." She picked up the thick paperback and closed it, losing her place. "It's really long and has these paragraphs I have to read a couple of times to understand them."

"But once you get through it the first time, you'll see what a great piece of literature it is."

"Maybe. You should tutor me in it." Violet's excitement about the prospect of her idea rose as she said her statement. "Yeah, I think I'd understand it quicker and like it more."

"That sounds fine, but not today. What about in a couple of days?"

Violet nodded. "Definitely before school starts."

"We have another week or so. Plenty of time."

Adam had nothing else to chat about and knew he better ask before he lost his nerve. "Listen, can I ask you something?"

Violet looked at him funny. "You've been talking to me for the last few minutes. Of course you can."

"Now, I don't know if you have one, but I wondered if I could borrow a digital camera. I don't own one and I need one for a day or two." He paused. "I know we haven't really talked a lot, but you're the only one I can ask. If you have one that is. I wasn't sure—"

Violet smiled. "It's okay, Adam, you can stop. I have one and yes, you can borrow it."

For some reason, Adam released a deep breath. "Oh, thank you so much."

"Let me go get it."

Violet bounced up the steps and disappeared into her house.

Adam was glad he came over to ask. He was glad he *did* ask since he was probably only minutes away from forgetting about it and walking away. Violet was nice and Adam was grateful for her allowing him to borrow it and even more grateful that she had a camera. Instead of teaching her the intricacies of *Moby Dick*, he'd have to make sure they took that bike ride he promised.

The front door opened and Violet came bouncing out just as she went in, with pep and happiness. She pressed some buttons as she approached.

"Now, promise me you won't look at any of the pictures on here," she said.

"I won't."

"They're boring anyway. Me and my friends just acting crazy."

"Why don't you delete them?"

"I haven't uploaded them to my computer yet." The camera beeped as she turned it off.

"I promise I won't." Of course, Adam had the urge to suddenly look at them. "I only need to take a couple of pictures."

"What kind of pictures?"

He was surprised the question took this long to be asked. "Well, I kinda don't want to tell you at the moment. I will, though. Just not now."

"Then I suppose I should ask you not to take naked pictures of yourself. Or at least if you do, don't leave them on the camera."

Adam heard the statement and saw a huge smile on her face. A joke. She was joking. Violet then threw out a laugh that made him want to kiss her and he thought she knew it as well. Her laugh faded into a girly chuckle and she darted her eyes from his mouth to his eyes. This happened three times, Adam counted, and he didn't know how to proceed.

If he should proceed.

She leaned forward—subtly, maybe an inch—and parted her lips just enough for Adam to notice. An earthquake-like flutter exploded in his stomach and he noticed his hands starting to shake. One of his legs—he couldn't tell which one—buckled slightly, forcing him to catch himself with the other leg.

Violet noticed. "It's okay Adam. I just want a kiss."

Her hands lifted to the top half of his arms, her touch sending an insane amount of jolts through his body. The feeling traveled quickly through his torso and stomach and ended up in the crotch. Adam was getting an erection and Violet was too close not to notice if this went on. She moved closer and Adam saw her shirt-covered breasts caress his shirt and below that, the tiny hairs all over his body perked at the thought.

Smiling, Violet lifted Adam's chin back up to her face. "My lips are up here."

Then she closed her eyes and pulled Adam into her, their lips pushing against each other. The warmth in his groin lessened, but that was because Violet had absorbed some of the heat with her own jeans. She had to know his erection was full by now. She just *had* to know. If she didn't she refused to adjust her body to compensate or she just didn't care.

Hot air passed between them through their mouths and Adam closed his eyes. His hands naturally cupped her back, though he did it awkwardly.

Five or six seconds later—Adam really didn't know how long the kissed lasted—Violet broke apart and opened her eyes. She still smiled at him, which Adam took as a good sign. Another few seconds later, she wasn't touching him anymore and this made Adam want her touch in a more intense way.

But that had to wait.

"Not bad, Adam," she said. "Not bad at all."

"That was nice."

"I agree."

She backed away, expertly navigating her steps. "Now don't forget about that bike ride," she said. "I want one before the school starts."

"You'll get one," he said. And he meant it too.

He waved back to her as he jumped on his bike and started back home.

CHAPTER SIXTEEN

That same night, about 3 a.m.

The angry grunts woke Adam and Tommy from sleep.

"What was that?" Tommy whispered.

"Don't know. *Shhh.*"

Outside, the wind blew by in varied blasts, whipping through the trees with unprotected abandon. It knocked on the window, wanting to be let in and Adam thought the glass would crack and come crashing in at any moment.

"Maybe it's the wind," Adam said.

"I heard growling. Like that day with Victor."

Adam had heard it too and really didn't want to admit it too himself. That meant the beast was too real, that the morning with Victor actually happened. *Just another confirmation*, he supposed.

The grunts continued in pulsed bursts: not loud, just deep and vibrating. Adam placed his hand on the wall closest to him and felt the sound waves traveling along the wood and plaster. A door opened and then shut. His father.

Adam quietly grasped the doorknob to his bedroom door and eased it opened. A small creak, like the sad cry of a cat, almost gave his antics away, but when Adam looked through the tiny crack, he saw his father turning the corner. *No time to see if anyone's watching; just got to take care of the grunts.*

"Stay here," Adam told Tommy.

Tommy said nothing.

Adam crept from the bedroom and lightly shut the door closed behind him. He paused, listening for any other sound besides the animal-like grunts. Any other sound to indicate his dad would come rushing around the corner, the heat of anger aimed right at him.

Another door opened and Adam assumed it was the golden door. He snuck to the end of the wall and poked his head around the corner in time to see the golden door snap shut.

"Hey," Tommy whispered.

Behind him, Adam flipped his hand back into the bedroom. "I said to stay there."

"I know, but I'm scared."

Turning around, Adam said, "Fine, but go no further than here—" He pointed to his own spot. "—when I go down the hall."

Tommy eyes widened. "You're going to the door?"

"Yes. I want to hear."

Adam eased out into the hall, careful to keep his steps silent. Halfway down, he looked back and saw Tommy poking his head out from the wall. His brother gave Adam a thumbs up sign and Adam nodded. *Please stay there,* Adam wished.

The golden door—in the few times Adam's seen it—had begun to chip and fade already. When did his dad paint it? Last week? Two weeks ago? Either he bought cheap paint or did a shoddy job. Minute cracks in random spots gave the door an antique appearance and Adam saw little chips of paint finding a new home on the floor. As he approached the door, Adam saw a dim outline of a footprint on the right side of the jamb. *I'm Victor's footprint,* it said, *remember me? Remember that day? He pressed me hard into the wood, but he didn't make it, did he?*

A deafening grunt shook the door, rattling the doorknob. Adam stopped, nearly jumping into the wall. Looking back again, Tommy had retreated into the adjacent hallway, maybe even back to his room.

Then a voice. A human voice, with words.

Adam couldn't make out the words, but he thought it sounded like his dad. He eased to the door and pressed an ear to the wood. The door emanated intense heat without burning his skin, as if he was holding a hand over the electric burners of the stove. He moved his head back an inch.

"This is too much," Adam heard through the door. "I can't."

A series of angry grunts followed.

"No."

A single grunt crescendoed into something barely tolerable and quickly subsided. Adam then heard the springs of the bed giving way, as if something heavy just removed itself and lightened the mattress' load.

"Stay away." Through the door again.

The next grunt started mad, but soon turned into what Adam thought was chuckling or outright laughter. Shuffled movement bounced along the floor and Adam felt the vibration on this side of the door. He glanced down and saw he was jumping mere centimeters off the wooden slats.

A low-pitched scream came through, jerking Adam a few feet. *What was going on in there?*

Adam knelt and pressed his cheek into the floor as best he could in order to see under the door. As he suspected, he only saw dark. Maybe a small dot of light from the glare of the moon or a flashlight, but he couldn't be sure.

"Let go of me!"

The sounds were clearer down here.

And louder.

"I'm not doing it I said!" It was definitely his dad. He sounded afraid.

Rhythmic grunts soiled the air. Adam smelled a stink he couldn't put together. He remembered his mother's last day, how the room smelled like beer, rotten meat and rose petals. It would have been absolute paradise if he could have those smells again—especially the rose petals—instead of this foul, moldy aura that could melt steel. Adam felt the hairs in his nose and on his head shriveling up and dying. The charring smell gave him a crazy shiver that rattled every bone he could think of.

Something crashed against the door. Shards of glass spilled from under the door into the hallway, one or two hitting Adam near his mouth. A different smell took away the bad one.

His mother's perfume.

He instantly recognized the glass from the perfume bottle. Closing his eyes, Adam saw it there on the nightstand, ready for another use by his mother. But now, some of the bottle lay shattered at his feet, like a snow storm of tears.

"Fine!" Adam heard the muffled voice of his father forcing its way through the door. "I'll do it just once more! And then that's it!"

The grunts turned happy—*if beastly sounds could turn happy*, Adam thought—and another set of shuffling sounds turned into a creaking bed. Whatever was holding his dad was now back in bed, ready for whatever his dad was doing just once more.

The doorknob jiggled and Adam knew immediately he should have been away from there the moment he heard the bed creak. It was already too late; he was already going to be caught so he stood there, facing the door.

A soft purr halted the jiggling doorknob.

"Yes, me too," Adam heard his father say.

Then a pause.

Adam took that opportunity to dash away, not caring if his feet made sounds that could wake the dead in the cemetery three miles away. He darted into his bedroom, flipping the door closed as he passed it. The door didn't shut all the way, instead stopping with an inch or two gap.

Tommy had returned to the bedroom. He sat huddled into the furthest reaches of his bed, pushed against the headboard. Any more pressure and Tommy would *become* the headboard.

"What did you see?" Tommy asked.

"*Shhh!* Dad's coming."

Tommy nodded. He slipped under his comforter and turned his head to the side, feigning sleep. Adam followed suit, keeping his eyes on his door.

Their father walked by, stopping at the door.

This is it, Adam thought. *He knew I was there. He knew I heard everything and is ready to come in here and switch me. Possibly switch me to death. Maybe that's the once more he heard his dad say.*

Adam took a deep breath and watched his dad's shadow reach for the door, then move away. Another second later, his dad was gone and heading down the stairs.

"That was close," Adam quietly said.

"Yeah. What did you see?"

"I didn't see anything, but I heard something weird."

"What?"

"Dad is going to do something. Whatever is in there, he's doing it for that thing."

"The thing that got Victor?"

"Probably."

"Did you see it?"

Adam shook his head. "I didn't open the door."

"Good. I'm glad you didn't. That monster would have gotten you."

"Which one? Dad or the thing?"

Tommy didn't have answer for that. Both of them knew two monsters lived in this house; one of them just happened to be their father.

Reaching under his pillow, Adam retrieved the digital camera. He turned it on and made sure the batteries registered full.

"What are you doing?" Tommy asked.

"Going to follow dad."

"That's crazy."

"I have to."

Adam watched Tommy contemplate all the bad things that could happen if they followed their father and all the bad things that has already happened. He watched Tommy grow up even a little more, if that was possible, when he said, "I'm coming with you."

"You don't have to. I'm just going to get some pictures. See what he's up to."

"I want to see."

Adam figured he couldn't talk his brother out of the decision so Adam just nodded. "Okay, but you have to be in charge of the flashlight."

Tommy pulled a flashlight from under his own pillow. "Already got one."

Smiling, Adam said, "Very good. You're already prepared."

They heard the back screen door spring open then clap shut. Adam had forgotten to lock that door, but he guessed it didn't matter anymore: his dad was one some kind mission.

Adam and Tommy scrambled to the window and watched their dad head into the shed and exit with a black garbage back. He threw it into the front seat and lowered the tailgate. He went back inside the shed and returned with a broom this time. With an impressive no-handed hop, their dad bounded into the bed of the truck and proceeded to sweep it out.

"What's he doing?"

"He's doing a little preparation himself is my guess."

Satisfied, their dad jumped down and tossed the broom near the shed. Then he got into the truck and tried to start it.

"Okay," Adam said quickly. "We have to move."

They ran from the room and as they leapt down the stairs, Tommy asked, "How are we going to keep up with the truck?"

"Common sense."

Another few breaths and then Tommy asked, "I don't get it."

"Don't worry about it right now."

They heard the truck start when they reached the back door, and then sputter out. A shot rang out.

"What was that!" Tommy yelled.

"Backfire. The truck won't start."

Tommy calmed down. "That's good, right?"

"Maybe, maybe not." Adam watched the truck carefully.

Their dad got out and lifted the hood. He tinkered with something for a few minutes and then slammed the hood down. Adam thought he heard cursing and smiled. *The truck won't start at all tonight and he doesn't have time to fix it,* Adam thought.

But is he coming back inside? The fearful part of Adam's mind offered. *He's probably just going to come back in here and forget he was going to do anything tonight.*

That part of his mind was wrong.

Their dad stood at the side of the truck, thinking about something and looking around. For a moment he looked lost, like a kid missing his parents in a department store, eyes wide, and lips pursed, ready to cry. The crying part probably wouldn't happen, but he definitely looked lost.

Then something near the oak tree caught his eye. Adam followed the gaze and saw his bike propped up against the trunk of the tree.

"No," he whispered.

Tommy tugged at Adam's arm. "No, what?"

"My bike."

Before getting the bike, their father disappeared into the shed once again and returned with a rolled up rope wrapped around his shoulder and armpit. Next, he snatched the garbage bag from the truck. A smile crossed his face as he approached the bicycle. He pulled the bike away from the tree and lifted a leg over the crossbar. Adam thought his father looked clueless to the operation of the bike, which made him snicker inside.

His father stuffed the bag into his shirt and sat on the seat, putting one foot on the pedal. He seemed uncomfortable on the bike and Adam wondered the last time his dad had ridden one.

But something came to him and he pushed the pedal and whisked forward. He brought his other foot to the opposite pedal and pushed with that one as well. *A little wobbly,* Adam thought, *but he's doing to do it.*

When their dad left the boundaries of the yard, Adam pulled Tommy through the door.

"We have to go," Adam said.

Tommy clicked on the flashlight and Adam stopped and put his hand over the end, smothering the light.

"Not now. Put it in your pocket."

The moon gave off enough light to see by; they probably wouldn't need the flashlight at all. Adam waited for Tommy to replace the flashlight before continuing.

Because their dad was still getting his bearings on the bike—and Adam figured his dad wouldn't be riding smooth at all tonight—Adam and Tommy had no problem keeping up. When they made it to the street, they saw their dad go around the corner, unbalanced, and they had to trot so as not to lose him, but other than that, a brisk walk was good enough to keep their dad in sight.

The adjacent streetlight forced Adam and his brother to hunker behind bushes and large trees, dash ahead to the next bush or tree, and hunker down again. Adam didn't want to risk being seen so early before he took any pictures—if anything would happen so he *could* take any.

The path of their father remained a mystery. He headed downtown at one point, but two blocks later, when he turned down an alley, Adam gave up on that destination. With the alley dark, Adam and Tommy could stay against the garages for safety.

Near the last three-quarters section of the alley, their dad almost caught them.

Whether it was bike-riding inexperience on their dad's part or something that distracted him, Adam and Tommy saw their dad wobble the bike, becoming unbalanced, and tumble to the ground. Luckily, he launched himself far enough so the bike didn't land on top of him, but he still rolled into the closest garage door. The door rattled, sending neighboring dogs into fits of barking rage. He looked up and stood, doing an injury check. From their position, Adam saw a few rips in their dad's clothes, but he looked relatively alright.

Adam was more concerned with the bike's health than anything.

His dad picked up the bike and looked down the part of the alley he just came from. *Maybe he thought something caused his fall,* Adam thought.

That wasn't it. For a moment, Adam swore his dad was looking right at them.

His dad flipped the kickstand down and took a few steps toward Adam and Tommy then stopped. "Hello?" He called out. "Who's there?"

He knows we're here, Adam's mind panicked. *He knows, he knows, he knows!*

"Who's there!? I saw you there!"

Adam planted his hand on Tommy's chest, holding him against the garage, knowing his brother might be frightened.

"You better not run!" With recklessness, their dad accelerated like no one Adam has seen before. He closed half the distance quickly before running out of breath.

Two driveways down, a garage door clunked and geared open, sending a loud, machine sound echoing between the garages. Their dad backed up a few feet when a tall man holding a shotgun emerged from the garage.

"What are you doing?" The man asked in a demanding way.

Their dad held up his hands. "Nothing. No problem here."

"You sent my Labs to crazytown with your yelling."

"I'm sorry," their dad said. "Just riding through the alley, that's all."

"At this time of night? What are you up to?"

"Nothing. Just getting my bike and leaving."

"Good."

"Have a good night."

The man swept the gun towards the end of the alley. "I will when you get outta here."

Their dad jogged to the bike, hopped on and sprinted out of the alley. The man watched him go before returning to the garage. When Adam heard the door closing and pitching the final thunk, he grabbed his brother and said, "Come on!"

They ran fast to the end of the alley and pivoted right, just in time to see their dad turning left on the next block.

Instead of following directly, Adam decided to continue down the alley across the street. If their luck continued, they should be able to catch a glimpse of their dad either crossing the street or making a turn.

He was right. When they stopped at the exit of the second alley, Adam peeked around the building and saw his dad continuing on. Of course, if his dad's path was straight on that street, then there was only one place he was headed; the only place that would make any sense at all.

CHAPTER SEVENTEEN

10 minutes later

Hydes Park sat on the extreme edge of town, on an entire block of the town that also contained the Little League baseball field and the High School's football field at one end of the park. The other end held six tennis courts in different degrees of appearance from recently painted to general decay. The tennis nets would probably be taken down in another month, so the wind, fall rain and snow couldn't do more damage since no one really took care of it.

In between the fields and the courts were the playground equipment and two basketball courts. The summer days found many kids and teenagers—and some adults—playing basketball and other kids enjoying the swings, slides and merry-go-rounds. The one unique thing that only seemed to be at this park was the lion water fountain. Because of the way the fountain was built, someone's head had to be inserted into the lion's mouth in order to drink from the faucet. Sounds gimmicky, but to Adam's surprise, the water was the best in town. Adam quickly tried to recall the numerous times he dared the plastic mouth in order to take a sip. As he grew older, the dares seemed stupid, but for a kid, the gaping, uninviting mouth was scary. The park also had a bandstand stage, which was only used during Labor Day festivities, when the town held its annual talent show.

Two lampposts lit the park: one near the basketball courts and another on the tennis courts. The other lights were reserved for the night baseball games. However, Adam knew the switch box with the light timers were located in the rear of the stage and also knew that someone could remove the padlock by unscrewing the hinge. Once or twice, he had to turn the lights back on when Tommy was at practice with this team so he was occasionally that someone.

Because Adam and Tommy came the back way, they entered the park by the tennis courts. Their dad came off of Oak Street, so he got into the park near the slides and basketball court.

To Adam, this was good. He and Tommy could hang by the tennis courts and keep an eye on their dad. But why the park? What was in the park that he would need a rope and a garbage bag?

Their dad leaned the bike against the lamppost and headed for the baseball field. He climbed over the chain-link fence. In another surprising move, he trotted across the ball field to the outfield fence and climbed over that. For some reason, he didn't look tired now. As their dad stood on the sidewalk, Adam and Tommy made their way to the left field fence to keep a closer eye on him.

Their dad's head swiveled left to right, searching the houses across the street for something. There was a new subdivision and it started on this street. Many of the house were recently built; much of the surrounding land was still in need of development.

Something pleased him and their dad headed for a chosen house. When he approached the yard, he crouched and continued to look side to side. He reached the left side of the house and then softly crept up the steps. At the front door, their dad checked the doorknob, but even in a small town like Seeton it was locked. Adam was glad it was locked. He had no clue what his dad's intentions were.

The camera!

Adam almost forgot. He dug the camera from his pocket and turned it on. The lens ejected and the rear screen blinked on, showing him a dark image of the ground. He pressed the flash button until it showed a lightning bolt in a NO symbol. Then, in a few quick strokes, he set the picture quality to the highest and found the shooting mode he wanted: NIGHT MODE. He was glad he practiced with the camera since borrowing it from Violet.

Aiming the camera to find his dad on the porch was harder. He had to find reference points and then move the lens to the house because his dad only showed up as a dark outline, which wouldn't allow the camera to focus properly. That was fine anyway because their father took his time with the door.

Adam snapped a couple of pictures. The first turned out pixilated and blurry, but once he allowed the camera to focus better, he could see his dad's back, the rope hanging from the shoulder and one of his hands wrapped in a thick cloth.

"I don't like this," Tommy said.

"Me neither, but we have to stay."

A sharp burst of glass breaking broke the night silence. Adam took a picture without looking. Looking across the street, Adam and Tommy saw their dad's hand reaching into the door.

"Is he breaking in there?" Tommy asked, amazed.

"Looks like it." *Click*. Another picture.

"I can't believe this."

Click.

A few seconds later, the front door of the house opened and their dad retracted his hand and unwrapped it, throwing the material in the garbage bag.

At that moment, an upstairs light flipped on. Adam pointed to it. "There," he said.

A silhouette crossed the path of light. Then another light turned on and another silhouette passed by.

"This is not good," Adam said.

Their father seemed unconcerned or oblivious to the lights and stepped inside—*click, click, click*—and shut the door. Then, a light on the first floor turned on, which looked like it was the room their dad just entered.

The scream came immediately.

"Did you hear that?" Tommy latched both of his hands on Adam's forearm.

"Yeah." It sounded like a woman. If they could hear it across the street, nearly half a block away, then surely the woman's neighbors could hear. Adam scanned the nearby houses; no lights turned on.

"Do you know who lives there?" Tommy asked.

"No. I don't know too many people in the new subdivision."

The shrill was immediately cut off and Adam stepped back from the fence. The terror he felt wracked his entire body and gave him a sickening, tingling sensation in his stomach, which sped through his bowels. He suddenly needed to go to the bathroom.

Click. Click.

"Let's go," Tommy said, a quiver emitting from his voice.

"Not yet."

"I don't like it here."

Adam sighed. "Then go by yourself."

"I'm scared."

"What do you have to be scared of? Dad's in there."

Tommy paused. "You know."

Adam did and he didn't blame Tommy one bit, but he didn't feel the pictures he'd taken so far were good enough. All they really showed were his dad entering the house of some woman and, as far as Adam could tell, she lived by herself. Any person with common sense would just assume his dad had a very late night date. That's all; no nefarious motives, just sex.

A little smile crossed Adam's lips, but it soon disappeared. His dad was not going for sex; he was going for something deeply sinister, Adam suspected.

"I'm sorry, Tommy, but just a little longer."

"I'm going to sit on that merry-go-round." Tommy pointed to the rusty metal unit that Adam was sure didn't spin smoothly anymore.

"Okay, but keep your eyes on me and don't go beyond that."

"I won't."

Adam returned his gaze to the only house on the block with a light on. He saw a couple of shadows in the view of the light converge into one faded blob. They struggled and soon, one of them slid down towards the floor. The remaining shadow left the frame of the window and Adam took another picture, even though it only showed the curtain and the light, and another one when his dad returned. He held something in his hand and his upper body bent over. Adam watched his father's shoulder twist and move in a strange way.

When blood splattered on the curtain, soaking it with its thick plasma, Adam whipped the camera up and zoomed in as far as he could and pressed the shutter as fast as he could. Blood continued to spray on the curtain. Through the camera lens, Adam watched the curtain wave with each mass of blood hitting the material.

His father sliced and cut for about five minutes before finally stopping. He then wiped his brow and pulled the garbage bag out of his shirt.

Click, click.

Things were happening too fast. Adam couldn't get enough pictures. The memory card told him he only had 25 pictures left to take. *That's okay,* he thought. He should wait and see if he can get additional pictures after his father left the house.

In a surprising move, Adam's father ripped down the curtain and stuffed it into the garbage bag. Then the shadow disappeared and the light on the first floor turned off and twenty seconds later, the upstairs light extinguished.

Adam dashed away from the fence and joined his brother by the merry-go-round. They hid behind the rusty metal and Adam waited for his father to exit the house.

"Can we go home now?" Tommy asked.

"Yes, but you're probably not going to like it there either."

The door to the house opened and their dad emerged, hauling the garbage bag behind him. No, he *dragged* the bag, as the weight seemed to slow him down. He used both hands and jerked the bag as if he was getting ready for the Hammer Throw that Adam had seen some of the track and fielders do. Down the steps his father went, the bag falling to the walkway. When he reached the street, he tried to lift the bag and with a lot of effort, he managed to do so, but Adam could tell the strain it placed on his father's perpetually injured foot from the squinting eyes.

Crossing the street caused no issues, but as his dad made his way back to the bike, he wondered how the trip back would go. How many times would he fall? The bag would give some major balancing issues and the ride over didn't go so well.

Click, click, click. Twenty-two left.

"Tommy," Adam said, "I want you to go home right now."

"Without you?"

"You'll just have a head start." Adam kept his eye on his father. "Get home and go into your room and lock the door."

"I don't want to go without you."

"I'll be there minutes after you."

"You promise?"

171

"Yes, but you have to promise—" Their dad reached the back fence of the field and flung the bag over. Adam heard a dull thump as it hit the outfield. "—to shut and lock the door and put the heaviest thing you can move in front of it."

"Like the bed?"

Adam nodded. "If you can move it."

His father made it halfway across the ball field. "Now go," Adam whispered loudly, but stopped Tommy with an afterthought. "Makes sure you unlock the front door. It's very important you do that."

Without another word—to Adam's relief—Tommy nodded and ran to the street and took off towards home.

At the first base fence, Adam's dad threw the bag over and hopped over as easily as he did before. He picked it up when he landed and moved rapidly over the basketball court to the bike.

First, his dad mounted the bike and balanced it between his legs. Then he reached down and picked up the bag, straining his back since he couldn't use his legs—which Adam knew from gym class was the best way to lift something heavy—and set it on the tiny dip on the handlebars. Holding one bag with the left hand and the right rubber grip of the handle with his right hand, his dad pushed off and placed both feet on the pedals.

The initial strokes were weak, almost sending the bike to the ground. The front wheel horrendously angled left and right and the bag threatened to fall from the handlebars. When his dad neared the street, he had it under control and had an even easier time when on the flat street. He seemed to do better with the weight of—

Adam's stomach sent bile up his throat. The hot, wet juice entered his mouth and he gagged, spitting it out on the merry-go-round. The fact Adam's mind immediately thought of a body made him cringe. Unfortunately, what else could be in that bag?

On the trip back, Adam made sure to stay in line with his dad a half of a block at a time. Adam hugged the lawns, keeping quiet so his dad wouldn't hear him and so Adam wouldn't wake anyone in the houses. Doing this was easy on the grass lawns, but when it came to crossing the street, he had to worry about rocks and sticks.

Between the park and home, Adam managed to take ten pictures. Twelve left.

When they hit their home street, Adam realized his father didn't falter on the bike one time. *Not once,* something inside him said. *That means he's enjoying his work. He wants to be careful of the new one so it doesn't fall and get bruised.*

His dad reached the house, Adam had to plan the next few minutes carefully. As predicted, Adam saw his dad ride into the back yard. That meant the front of the house was clear for five minutes at most.

Hopefully, Tommy had done what Adam had requested earlier.

Adam waited five more seconds and sprinted down the street, crossing their house's front lawn and bounded up the steps. Taking a deep breath, Adam wrapped his right hand around the doorknob and twisted.

Unlocked.

Adam looked up to the second bedroom and mouthed *Thank you, Tommy.*

He pushed the door open, jetted inside and shut the door. He listened for a second to make sure his dad wasn't in the house. When Adam heard the cellar doors snapping shut, he ran up the stairs taking them two at a time.

The bedroom door was shut. Adam gripped the doorknob and pushed the door open, but it thumped against something wooden. *Tommy listened well tonight*, Adam thought.

"Hey Tommy," Adam whispered.

At first, there was no answer. Soon, light shuffling made its way to the door.

"Adam?"

"Yeah, it's me."

"Hold on. Let me move the chair."

Tommy slid a chair—probably the chair Adam enjoyed reading on—and it squeaked along the floor. His brother pushed it for about twenty seconds in quick shoves. When he thought both Tommy and the chair were far enough away, Adam opened the door. Tommy stood up from the chair, which *was* the reading chair Adam loved.

"I was worried," Tommy said.

"It wasn't that long. I'm here."

"I know."

"Now quiet. He's coming in a minute."

Tommy jumped into his bed and pulled the covers up to his neck and closed his eyes. Adam did the same.

The hall light came on and Adam heard his father's footsteps followed by a dragging sound. Plastic on wood. The garbage bag on the hallway floor. Without looking, Adam knew that's what it was.

Step, drag, step, drag, step, drag, step drag.

A doorknob shook and then Adam and Tommy heard the golden door opening and they frightfully looked at each other.

Adam shot out of bed, camera in hand, and snuck to the corner of the hallway. He clicked the shutter and saw the flash icon blinking.

The flash, the flash, the flash!

Adam quickly turned the camera off. He forgot to change the settings when the camera shut of automatically. All the default modes—including auto-flash—came back to life. *That was a close one there, Adam. The flash almost gave you away.*

It was true, no matter how he looked at it.

With his dad behind the golden door, there was no way Adam could capture any proof. What he had was stronger than the last time he thought about it: his dad going inside, the woman screaming, blood on the curtain, his dad leaving with a heavy garbage bag. That might be enough to get the cops over here, but may not be enough to get his dad arrested.

Adam tapped the camera in his hand. He had to think fast. Had to think of something that could prove his father killed—no, *murdered*—that woman. He remembered a book he read last year called *In Cold Blood* where two men decided to come together to commit mass murder for no particular reason than just to do it. Since they weren't able to commit the murder on their own, their teamwork ultimately managed to complete the task. They were caught and tried, but the story always stuck with Adam, mainly because it could have been any two people in the world that got together to kill.

Was his dad part of a couplet? Why did he drag the bag all the way to the bedroom?

Adam knew now that he had to get into the bedroom and see for himself what was going on. It was dangerous, but it had to be done.

For his sake.

For Tommy's.

CHAPTER EIGHTEEN

Five minutes later

Adam returned to his bedroom. Tommy still lied under the bed sheets, but his eyes were open now.

"I need to tell you something, Tommy."

His brother sat up.

Adam needed to get this out fast. "I'm going into the room."

"No!"

"I have to. Whatever is going on in there, I have to see." Adam stood and Tommy grabbed onto Adam's shirt. "Tommy, let go."

"Are you going to stop him? It?"

"I don't think I can," Adam answered. "That beast and dad in the same room is too much for me to handle. I just want to nab a few pictures."

"Why don't we just call the police? That officer that came the other day."

Adam shook his head. "If he believed anything that day, he would have returned here to check things out again. Obviously—" Adam calmed down. "I don't have time for this."

Tommy started to cry. Tears rolled down his cheeks in droves, dripping onto his bed sheets. A tiny whimper came, but to Tommy's credit, the sound stayed pretty quiet. Adam started to say something else, something to console his brother, but it would be no use: he was going into the room whether Tommy liked it or not.

Adam didn't even like it.

"Lay down," Adam whispered.

"I wish mom was here to read to me," blubbered Tommy.

Adam tugged the covers to his brother's neck and gave him a peck on the forehead.

"No matter what happens," Adam said. "Stay right here."

Amidst tears and a want to pull Adam into bed with him to stop him from going, Tommy nodded.

"Thank you," Adam said.

Adam left the bedroom, closing the door all the way behind him.

The hallway seemed dimmer somehow or maybe that was the air. Could air be dim? Adam thought maybe the air *seemed* thicker and a feeling of impending doom erupted in his legs. He took the four steps from his bedroom door to the corner and looked around it. At the end of the hallway, at the golden door, was an aura of darkness. A black-gray fog swirled from under the door, rising to the ceiling like a barrier meant to frighten him.

The golden door sat blurry and unrecognizable from the previous days.

The fog was doing its job, scaring him. Adam stared at the constantly imploding mist and wondered how he thought this was a good idea. Moving through the fog meant he would have to open the door. Opening the door meant he would have to go in. Going in meant he would have to see his dad, a dead woman and a beast. And seeing them would mean—

He didn't know what that meant.

From the other side of the door, he heard his dad mumble something, which was answered by a bowel-moving grunt. Additional fog came spilling out from the crack at the bottom of the door, expanding the wall another few inches towards him.

Sucking in a breath of air, Adam pushed forward down the hall, stopping when he reached the edge of the fog. Another growl from inside; more fog out here.

Adam jabbed his finger into the fog, pulling back, expecting a shock of some sort. None came. The smoke-like haze was warm, almost inviting, and created a space for his finger, surrounding it immediately. A small, burnt meat smell—like when his father charred hamburgers on the grill—found its way to Adam's nose.

Satisfied it was harmless, Adam reached through and gripped the doorknob. Another mumble from his dad followed by a low roar made Adam jump. The roar died down quickly and became a beastly purr bordering on natural breathing.

Adam returned his hand to the knob, turned it and shoved the door open. The site before him sent his heart into palpitations and took his breath.

CHAPTER NINETEEN

Immediately After

Time slowed to a syrupy crawl as Adam peered inside the bedroom at his father, who was holding the garbage sack, and the creature, half-stopped from crawling out of the bed. But something was familiar to Adam about this…this *thing* as it hung over the edge of the bed, glaring at him with anger. It wasn't the beast he, Tommy and Victor encountered days ago.

Well, not entirely.

The fog of anger spilled out into the hallway like an oven had been left on overnight, but the body portrayed a body missing something, something fragile. The creature was drastically less rough and its hands and arms actually looked comforting. The rest of the body, moving up from the torso, actually had a feminine look, as if at any moment this monster could turn into a woman.

Something human.

The face gave away the most telling attitude. Love.

Adam squinted his eyes, peering into the beast's. It looked at him with that same familiarity he sensed. The face appeared the most human of any part and when the creature smiled at him—and it was a complete smile—Adam suddenly knew who sat on the bed ten feet from him.

His mother.

The light had changed in the room since he last saw it. Adam was glad he could now see everything in the room and didn't question the reason.

At first glance, the beast didn't look like any human form, male or female and Adam didn't know if anyone other than someone extremely close—immediately family most likely—would know it was her. If he brought Tommy in here right now, would he know?

But there was one other person in the bedroom who knew.

His father.

He stood opposite the bed, near the writing desk his mother occasionally wrote letters on. His father's mouth widened, agape as the Grand Canyon. Was that more in shock he was caught in the bedroom or surprise that Adam lingered outside the door? Adam didn't care; it was only a matter of time and his father's time was up.

His father slumped, dropping the bag on the floor. At this moment it was empty. That was because the previous contents of the bag were spilled all over the bedroom floor. Adam saw an arm, a couple of fingers and two legs. The other arm remained attached to the torso, which sat halfway under the bed. Adam didn't see a head and he could take one guess where that head was.

I'll give you three guesses, his mind said, *the first two don't count!*

"What are you doing!?" His father bellowed.

Adam didn't say a word. He took a step inside the bedroom and shut the door behind him.

"That's fine," his father said. "She will feed well tonight."

"I can't believe you're doing this!" Adam screamed.

Shrugging, his father said, "No need to scream at me. It's her you need to talk to." To make sure Adam knew he was talking about the beast, his dad picked up the woman's free arm and tossed it to the monster/mom.

Her reaction was quick: her hand snatched the bloody and pale arm out of the air like a frog's tongue snatching a fly. In another swift motion, the beast/mother bit off the end near the elbow like a piece of celery, with a louder, elongated crunching sound. The face squashed and she threw the arm back at Adam's dad.

A few grunts came from her slobbering mouth, but Adam was able to make out the words *bitter* and *something fresh.*

"Is that mom?!"Adam asked. He already knew the answer, but he had an overwhelming urge to seek the confirmation.

"I think you already know that answer." his father replied, turning around and grabbing an axe.

Adam raised his camera.

Four pictures; eight left.

The flash lit up the room like a strobe light, shining on the walls, his dad, the floor (which Adam noticed had been waxed recently), the bed and the monster/mom. While the flash surprised his dad, he

182

simply blocked his eyes with his hands; the beast screamed in agony, diving into the bed for cover. Even the muffled screams shook and vibrated the bed and walls.

So the light hurts it, Adam thought.

"Are you taking pictures?" His dad dove for Adam, aiming for the camera, but Adam easily scooted to the side and hopped over the haphazardly strewn limbs. His dad slipped and slammed into the dresser.

A sinking feeling overcame Adam; he didn't like being away from the only escape route. He shot a quick glance to the window; the ground looked miles away. If he had to he could go through the window, but the fall would severely hurt him.

"Give me the camera," his father demanded.

The hairy atrocity turned over, attempting to leave the bed.

"No. What you are doing is terrible! How many have you killed? Two that I know of. One that I can prove!" Adam was spouting now. "And why? Why are you killing people? Do you enjoy it?! Does your penis get hard thinking about it?"

The last question sent his father into a rage and Adam didn't know why he said it. His father was on him before Adam could do anything. They both tumbled to the ground, his dad pinning him to the floor, straddling Adam's arms to his sides.

The beast made it off the bed and slid along, wiggling slowly like a snake.

Adam felt the weight and shape of the camera still in his hand. How had he held onto it with the impact? No time for an answer: his dad grabbed hold of Adam's neck. A small tuft of air immediately left.

Strangled by your dad, his mind said. *No chance to put up a fight. You did all this tonight for nothing. You couldn't save yourself and you couldn't save Tommy.*

"Tommy," Adam gasped through the loss of air.

"That's right, Tommy," his father said. "After you, Tommy."

His father squeezed harder and Adam's body took over, squirming and bucking to get an arm free, to loosen the grip on the neck so more air could get in, to get the fight or flight response in high gear.

Adam looked into his father's eyes. If he couldn't say anything else, he would at least try to make his dad see the last minute of his son's life.

But his dad was crying.

This surprise made Adam stop moving.

Adam's body went limp at the same moment he saw the beast tower over both him and his father. For a split second, the thing looked more like his mom than a mean, uncaring beast. For that split second, waves of longing flowed over Adam's body and he instinctively reached out for her, but his arms were contained and he could only feel like he reached for her.

Two pale green arms raised high above his father's head and Adam watched them lower their heavy muscle directly onto the crown of his dad's head. Surprise found its way to his eyes as they went wide. His grip loosened and the legs weakened, allowing Adam to finally free his arms. He thought about launching a fist into his dad's face, but it didn't really matter since Adam watched his dad's eyes roll into his head and he flopped onto the floor unconscious.

"Dad?"

Adam scrambled to his knees and checked his dad's pulse. Weak, but still pumping. He looked at the beast. "Look what you've done!"

The grunt that responded came softly from the thing's throat. Not angry or crazy, but confused. She made a motion with her arms that indicated she might approach him, but before that could happen, Adam backpedaled like a crab to the window. The mass of the monster/mother blocked the doorway and almost any available light that attempted to get in.

"*Graaaawweeeew,*" the unsightly thing cooed. It decided to move towards Adam anyway.

His dad stirred, groaning.

The beast paused, her head tilting down towards his dad. Adam immediately saw the intention swimming from her eyes. She appeared gleeful about the prospect of this one. Forget about the stale woman recently brought in here, his dad lied on the floor, fresh, his skin still teeming with life.

"*Greeeaaaaw,*" this time. A radiant grunt of want.

The needy monster bent down towards his dad, saliva dripping like a waterfall on the floor and his dad's clothes, soaking in dark circles. Adam tried to stand, to maybe dart out of here, but strength hadn't reestablished itself in his limbs. They still shook, as if his whole body was nervous and taking it out on his arms and legs. Next to him, he saw an open, facedown hardback book lying on the floor next to the chair his father was sitting in when he came to see his mom on her last day. The dust jacket had long been removed and he couldn't see the title, but saw the book was thick, thicker than what he would ever figure his dad to read.

Adam reached over and grabbed it. The book shut, losing its place. He cocked the book in his arm like he was preparing to throw a baseball and happened to catch the title: *Moby Dick.*

His favorite book. *Moby Dick?* Adam's brain questioned the reason his father was reading *Moby Dick.* Was he reading for pleasure? Probably not. Was he reading it to learn something about what literature was? Probably not. Was he trying to improve his reading comprehension? *If he wanted to do that,* Adam thought, *there was nothing better than Moby Dick.* But probably not. Was he reading it for—

Adam knew the reason. The reason—

Continuing with his plan, he launched the book at the creature, aiming for the head, hoping it would hit it anywhere, distracting it. The book flew through the air, end over end, finally smacking the beast on its deformed and puss-bubbled ear. Its head whipped to the side; its horrendous yell communicating how much pain the book delivered, which was probably enhanced by any original pain it already had.

She glared at Adam and methodically rubbed her ear. Unfortunately, she resumed her death-lust for his father.

With speed inconsistent with the previous motions or even the previous ten minutes, the monster's hand dropped to his father's neck. She squeezed it like his father had just squeezed Adam's neck. Suddenly, his dad's face realized what was happening and he lifted his head up as far as he could. The eyes, however, told a different story: *just letting you know we are still under the weather from that hit. We are a little blurry and we are going to let you see or allow you to stand until we are good and ready.*

Seconds later, his dad's face grew pale. Both eyes started giving up resistance and protruded from their sockets, trying to relieve pressure. Except when Adam heard tiny bones crunching, like the sound of corn kernels smashing together when walked over, he knew it was too late. Too late for his dad to save himself.

Too late for Adam to save his dad. So far, he was two for two in the not-saving-family-members department.

His mother—*not mother, monster,* Adam thought—dipped her head down and released her fingers at the same time her mouth opened. It opened wide enough to wrap most of it around his father's neck. The lips pulled back and quivered as the thing tasted the sweat glistening on the neck skin. Teeth stuck out, hesitating slightly before taking a huge, bloody bite of his father's neck.

Skin and muscle drew taut and then snapped as the beat pulled up. She swallowed without chewing and went in for seconds. Blood squirted in every direction, some of it landing on Adam's pant leg. He drew back the leg.

"Stop!" he yelled at the beast.

Adam stood, using the windowsill to push against. He felt strong and just assumed his body requested some adrenaline.

The hand of sausage fingers emerged from nowhere and raked his dad's back, tearing clothes and exposing muscle and lower levels of epidermis and portions of the spine. The hand acted as a grater from his dad's lower butt all the way to the bitten portion of the neck. She brought her hand to her mouth and licked each finger clean, like Adam and Tommy usually did when they ate the greasy chicken from the grocery store.

The slurps echoed in Adam's head and the human meat from his father elicited a satisfying, long grunt from the beast.

Adam turned his body to the side and unlocked the window. He stuck his fingers into the lift holes and tugged. The window slid upwards easier than expected. Cool, night air drifted inside, chilling his skin. He didn't know if he could make it to the bedroom door and he didn't know if he could make it to the ground. Well, he could make it to the ground simple enough: a straight shot down this way or a not-so-straight shot around his father and the creature to the door. Adam thought for only a second.

He draped his right leg over the windowsill. His foot connected with a ledge he never noticed before. A quick feel with his toes said the ledge might be six inches wide or maybe a little more. *That's good.*

Keeping an eye on his monster/mom, he gripped the side of the window, summoning the courage to leap to the ground. He counted to three and as he pulled himself with his arms and pushed on the skinny ledge with his feet, a powerful hand found its way into the band of his jeans.

His movement stifled, Adam turned his head and saw the aberration directly behind, binding him with her grotesque hand. Adam attempted another shift forward, but her hold was too strong. Adam felt himself being pulled back into the room. He used everything inside of him to stay locked in the window in hopes the grip would break and he could leap to the ground.

Seconds later, he found himself falling backwards, landing on the bedroom floor. Adam twisted immediately, jumping to his feet. And that's when the change started.

The thing took a step back, holding its face. Its eyes closed and then opened extremely wide; so wide that Adam though the scaly eyelids would disappear into the head. A hoarse roar pounded Adam's ears. Some of the skin bubbled and vibrated as tufts of hair detached and floated to the floor. Even a few pieces of skin slid off like pancakes going down a slide of syrup. Strings of gross tendons tried to hold on, but the skin broke free, slapping against the floor.

It tried to hold onto the bed for support, but its legs gave out. The monster fell to its knees, still holding her face. Adam could only see cheekbones and ears, which surprisingly were slowly forming into something else. Something more *human.*

Another phenomenal grunt. *"Grrrreeeeeelp!"*

Was that 'help'? Adam wondered. *Was the beast/mother asking for help?* No, it couldn't be. Whatever was happening to it wasn't anything he could help with anyway.

Adam saw a chance as the monster roared and screamed and grunted things that would probably haunt him for years. He would wake up in the middle of the night, remembering this moment, this night as sweat soaked his pillows. How did it go in the movies? He would seek out a psychiatrist to help him with his nightmares and be put on some kind of medication that would calm him. Or make him paranoid. *That's how it always is in the movies. The main character is always paranoid. Looking over his shoulder. Thinking the monster that almost killed him in his youth was always behind him.* His relationships would suck as well. With no chance of sustaining a girlfriend or lover or wife, he'd resort to drinking. Drinking the hard stuff at that. He would probably become a writer, using this experience to draw on the fears of others to sell books. This would be all the woman he would need. The love of the printed page; the love of pouring part of your soul out for others to wonder what made you like this; the love of story. Inevitably, this would drive him insane and he'd wander the streets drunk and fall on the street, hitting his head on the concrete and dying, like Edgar Allan Poe.

A sound unlike anything heard before shook Adam out of the thoughts of his perceived futures.

The open path from the window to the door set Adam in motion. He accelerated as fast as his legs would allow. The door came closer and closer, like he was zooming in with a camera lens—

He forgot about the camera!

It wasn't in his hands and he checked his pockets. Nothing. *He needed that camera.* About halfway to the door, he looked behind him. The camera sat innocently under the window, beckoning to be saved. *Don't leave me here! You need me! All those pictures you took are inside; if someone doesn't see them, no one will believe all this happened!*

"I know!" Adam yelled back.

He unconsciously slowed as he passed the beast. She looked differently now, something unknown rejuvenating her body. But there was no time to dwell on the newly formed features, which were still shaping into something Adam couldn't make out.

The door seemed so close now and Adam pushed his legs harder, wanting to sprint the final distance. He felt something wrapping around his ankle, yanking ferociously. His right leg flipped backward from under him and his other leg slipped, still trying to find traction. Adam went still like a stone and fell flat on his face. At the last second, he turned his head to the side, making his cheek and temple take most of the impact. The sudden pain wasn't so bad and Adam knew he was lucky he didn't break a nose or knock out half his teeth.

Adam rolled on his back, knowing what had hold of him.

Except it wasn't the monster that had him.

It was his mom.

Deep in the back of his head, Adam knew that his mom wasn't holding him. In some way it was, but Adam knew who she was before this…this *thing* before him came to be.

Most everything about this newer creature resembled his mom in human form. The dark hair; the pale, creamy skin; the thin nose; the amber eyes: everything suggested that Adam was staring up at his mom. Everything else told Adam this was the beast, the monster that enjoyed eating people. *Feeding* off of people.

"I'm so glad you're here, Adam," the mom-thing said. "I've missed you."

Adam tried to push away and shake his leg free, but she had a tight hold; Adam realized that most of her limbs still remained in old form. In fact, she squeezed tighter and Adam stopped for fear his ankle bone would snap.

"What's your hurry? Gotta go see that bitch, Violet?"

A crazy, nervous jolt sent Adam reeling. "Let me go!" He yelled.

She shook her head. "No way. I need you, Adam. You're not going anywhere."

"What do you need me for?"

"I'm hungry. I need you to feed me."

Feed her? "How am I supposed to feed you?" Adam hoped that keeping the conversation active, she'd release her grip a little and he could break free.

"Well," she tipped her head in his dad's direction, "since your dad is not doing so well, I need someone to *feed me.*"

"Not doing well? He's dead!"

"I had to save you. He was going to kill you and give you to me and I promised you I'd never let him hurt you again." A few *tsks* found their way out of her mouth. "Besides, he wasn't bringing me any good ones lately. The ones with the hot blood who try to fight when they know their last breath is seconds away. Those are the tastiest; *those are the best.*"

Adam focused on the hold; it still remained steadfast.

"And now that I've saved you, I need you to bring me the good ones."

"No."

That simple answer caused his mom's eyebrows to furrow. The grip didn't loosen as he'd hoped, but became tighter. Another squeeze and his ankle bone would crack like a hammer to ice.

"You're hurting me!" Adam pleaded.

"Because you're not cooperating with mommy."

Adam dug his voice around the pain. "You're not my mommy."

The mom-beast pulled Adam hard by the ankle. Something snapped horribly and a thousand snakes of pain told his brain that the ankle bone was broken or that a muscle tendon had given out. He hoped the latter, but either way, he was uncomfortably prone underneath the beast.

"I'm sorry to hear that, Adam. I didn't want you to be a victim. Ever."

With little effort, she raised his leg up, intending to start feeding there. Adam wondered how long it would take her to eat him. An hour? A few minutes? What would she go after when she finished with the leg? Would she find him repulsive since he didn't *try to fight when he knew his last breath was seconds away?* Maybe she'd leave him be to relax here with his dad and their new friend, the blonde woman.

"How did Victor taste?" The question halted his mom's movement.

A dastardly smile crosses his mom's lips and this made her look less like his mother. Her teeth chomped a few times in satisfaction of the memory. "Oh, he tasted just great. The fear I felt dripping onto my tongue made me want more like him. He tried to fight near the end—like I usually like them—but his fight was also wrought with fear."

She looked up, the memory seemingly floating there. "Yes, Victor was good." Her eyes cast down into his. "But you don't appear to have this fear he had and you don't appear to have the fight either. I don't think you'll taste as good as some of the others. I am curious about it though, since you are my son."

"How did you get like this? I don't understand?"

She gave him a hearty laugh from deep within her being. "Don't even try to understand, Adam. Something evil heard my promise and only required death in payment."

"You could have said no. You could have just kept me and Tommy company in our hearts. Maybe that's all we needed. We didn't need you to turn into this." Adam gave his leg and small tug and it released a little. *Good, keep her talking.*

"Then your father would have continued to hurt you! And I couldn't have that!"

"He never hurt us that bad. He didn't *switch* us all the time."

"And why do you think that is? Do you want something like this on you?" She pulled down the nightgown from her shoulder—exactly the same way she did that first moment in the bedroom—with her free hand. The gash was still there, except it had grown, like it *was* the shoulder and not a wound any more. Adam could see into the cut, dark red blood oozing and running down her arm. She pinched the skin around the cut like she was popping a pimple and laughed with a partial grunt and human sound. Blood squirted on her face and neck and some even made it to Adam's shirt. The mom-beast's tongue darted out and swerved to find the little dots of blood.

The hold loosened some more. "But you don't know if he would have hurt us if you weren't—" Adam tried to come up with a word. All he could say was, "—*like this.*"

"I am like this because I knew what drove your father. Fear kept him motivated. Oh, he tried once or twice to get away from here, from me and this place, but you'd be surprised what else evil will allow you to do. He thought by going to Chicago that I wouldn't find him, but I did. I found him holed up in some crappy building with some homeless people. Let me tell you something about homeless people: they don't taste good at all. Dirt, Adam. They taste like dirt. So I promised to keep you safe by keeping him here doing what I needed to be alive to fulfill my promise. And as you can see, promise kept."

Adam glanced at her hand around his ankle. Even though he saw it there, he didn't *feel* it there. "I wish you hadn't made that promise so those my father needed—no, forced to kill—would still be alive. I see it now—" He really did see it now. His mother made him do those things. Sure, his dad could have said no, but he didn't. He was protecting Adam and Tommy from her rather than her protecting them from their dad. "You made him do those things."

With a surprised twist, Adam got away from the grip. He crawled away, eventually popping up to his feet, ready to burst through the door. The mother-monster had beaten him and stood in his path.

"Adam, just relax. It is going to happen." Her face shimmered for a moment. The normal, human skin gave way to the monster skin and back again. "I have to."

The window, his brain reminded. *And don't forget the camera. It's right there.*

Adam turned, ready to make a dash out through the window and into the night air.

"Are you okay, Adam. I heard—" Adam's eyes closed when he heard Tommy's voice.

"Adam!" His brother screamed, terrified.

CHAPTER TWENTY

Immediately.

Adam and his mother saw Tommy at the exact same moment. The difference was while she slobbered globs of spit from hunger, Adam started shaking from not knowing what to do. He summoned all the synapses in his brain to fire and quickly come up with a solution to the problem before him. *The problem: Tommy in the doorway, his ugly and fast beast-mother between him and Tommy. The solution?*

"I don't know," Adam whispered to himself.

"Mommy?" Tommy questioned.

He's seen her, Adam thought.

"It's not her!" Adam screamed. "It's still the monster!"

Adam saw the confusion on his brother's face. He looked from his mother-beast to Adam, probably in wonder at the former and disbelief at the latter. Adam knew he had to act fast or Tommy would probably get hurt.

"Tommy," his mother cooed. "I'm so glad you're here too. My two boys."

To Adam's horror, Tommy took a step inside the bedroom. Then another. And another. When he was beyond bedroom door, the beast-mother opened her mouth and released an earth-shattering roar. The house's windows rattled and Adam felt the floor vibrate and he feared it would collapse. He feared the entire house would collapse. Outside, leaves fell from the trees and his bike, which appeared to have been lovingly propped against the tree by his dad, fell over.

As he lied there feeling the sound through is body, especially his heart—he had to catch his breath twice— the digital camera nuzzled his hand. Looking down, he saw the camera lightly bouncing into the side of his pinkie. He covered the camera with his hand and scooted it under him.

Unfortunately, Adam realized he shouldn't have taken the time to do that.

When he looked up, Tommy was being held by her; she stood behind with her arms wrapped around Tommy, like a big bear hug. A monster bear hug.

"Adam?" Tommy said, still confused. "Is this mom?"

Adam shook his head, the words not able to come.

The beast clumsily stroked Tommy's hair and then ran a monster finger down his cheek. Tommy started to cry, finally realizing he was in serious trouble. He started to struggle.

Adam jumped up, slipping the camera into his back pocket since he already had it, and made a move towards the creature that was his mom and beast at the same time and starting to fully turn back into the beast.

Strange enough, to Adam's curiosity, she remained stationary. When he reached the uncomfortable mom/son couple, the beast swung out her arm, hitting Adam hard in the chest. This knocked him into the bed. He flipped over the end, doing a backward somersault onto the mattress.

His chest burned, the pain seeping into the rest of his upper body. Adam sat up with no problem, thankful nothing broke.

The beast-monster-mother gave Adam a capricious smirk and dropped her lower jaw wide open. Two thoughts occurred to Adam: the first was it was too wide to open any further before it tore completely from the hinge and the second was that the opening was just wide enough.

Wide enough to surround Tommy's head.

Tommy eye's looked up, but he couldn't see the mom-creature lower her mouth onto the top of his head. Adam was sure he could feel her mouth on him. Tommy released a wail that Adam had never heard from him before. He wiggled, but that was making things worse. The mouth-grip held strong. Little streams of blood ran down Tommy's forehead and face, where each of her teeth had punctured him.

Her eyes tilted toward Adam and—*impossible, impossible, impossible*—her lips spread even further into a grotesque smile. She took one of Tommy's flailing arms and raised it at the elbow. Tommy stopped moving. The shock on his face and body told Adam he was giving up.

Like Victor did.

"*No!!!*" Adam yelled. "Keeping twisting, Tommy!"

He couldn't.

It only took another moment for the mom-beast to return back to its original form: matted, sweaty hair; green skin; thick fingers; atrocious-looking hands and feet. And all of her had Tommy to herself.

"Mom!" Adam tried to get its attention, but she had other thoughts.

She picked Tommy up and started to push him into her mouth. Adam had seen snakes at the zoo kind of do the same thing, gagging in a rat inches at a time. The creature was doing the same thing.

Tommy screamed in agony, in pain, in everything fearful in his entire nine years. Spiders, his dad, the past month, the death of Victor, reading thick books, math, his first grade teacher Mrs. Remington. All these things that Adam knew about and probably others he didn't.

The beast bit down on Tommy's head, a maddening crunch killing Adam's soul. Blood and bits of skull sprayed everywhere. When she lifted her head up to take another bite, chunks of brain fell to the floor. The beast enjoyed this. She *reveled*. The next bite wasn't so disgusting: she ripped a huge piece of Tommy's shoulder and swallowed it whole.

Adam tried to slide off the bed, but the searing pain in his chest obstructed his movement. He only managed to get his feet to the floor.

Adam looked at Tommy. His lifeless body, minus a portion of his head and shoulder, slumped to the floor, thudding continuously until his entire body lay at the beast's feet.

She grunted maniacally, turning to Adam.

"You killed Tommy!"

Without a care, she reached down and ripped off one of Tommy's leg. Her sharp teeth easily chopped through the flesh and bone as she swallowed it a section at a time. She looked at Adam the whole time.

Adam's face turned red; he could feel his blood getting hotter and hotter by the second. A new liquid flowed through his body: adrenaline. The dull thud in his chest disappeared and his arm muscles twitched as he clenches his fists around the bed sheets.

"*AAAAAAHHHHHHH!*" Adam stood, using the angry scream as motivation to move quickly. He propelled himself from the bed, bringing the sheets with him. He didn't know what he grabbed; he just hoped whatever he had would do what he wanted.

The sheets flowed behind him like a cape and this distracted the beast as Adam ran by it, draping the sheets over its head.

A roar told Adam that it didn't like what just happened.

Good, you old bitch. Dad was right about that part, wasn't he?

Adam kept running, aiming is path towards the bedroom door. This time, he was going to make it. He hurtled through the door, hearing a loud thump behind him. He stopped, turned around and saw the beast writhing on the floor, working the sheets of its body.

He shut the door and ran down the stairs.

CHAPTER TWENTY-ONE

Five minutes later

Adam could still hear the beast's consternation upstairs as he bolted through the back door. Without hesitation, he ran to the shed, which was already unlocked from his dad's previous night's discretions. He should have brought a flashlight.

Standing in the doorway, he emptied his mind and forced it to remember where everything was.

He pictured the inside of the shed easily enough, the layout simple. He slowly dropped different pieces of tools on the wall, toolboxes on the floor and various trinket drawers on the workbenches. Then, something else dropped into the picture, underneath the far workbench.

Walking slowly through the middle of the shed, he stopped when he thought he should have stopped: right in front of the bench. He bent down and reached under, feeling around a weedwacker, a smaller toolbox and a five-gallon bucket.

It's got to be here.

Moving his hand a foot to the right found the gas can. He removed it from its home, stood up and walked back through the shed and into the yard. He opened his eyes and still heard the muffled frustrations of the beast.

Good. She's still in there.

He shook the can. From the weight, he guessed the two-gallon can was about half-full, maybe a little fuller.

He ran back inside the house and opened one of the junk drawers in the kitchen. He rummaged until he found a box of matches. Adam was a little glad they weren't the book type because for some reason he always had a hard time with the flimsy ones, often burning the tip of his thumb when the sulfur sparked.

There were footsteps from above. The monster must have freed itself.

As he reached the top of the stairs, he heard slams against the golden door. *Blam! Blam! Blam!* Adam knew the door would soon break. The creature was heavy and strong.

Working fast, he whipped around the corner, removing the nozzle from the gas can. When he reached the golden door—additional paint chips falling to the floor with each thunderous hit—he jerked the can in every direction, dousing the door and the walls around it. Adam struck a match; it lit on the first try and he held it to one of the wet spots on the door.

The gas ignited softly, fire rolling up the door swiftly until it connected with the gas on the wall. In seconds, the entire end of the hallway was engulfed in flames. Adam stepped back, more from the heat than anything, and continued to splash gas on the floor. When he reached the corner to the adjacent hall, he struck another match and dropped it to the little drips of gas near his feet.

These flames traveled along the wooden floor to the fire on the door, and became one, as if in a strange fire-marriage.

The blasts against the golden door stopped. The beast was probably contemplating the source of the heat, trying to figure a way out. Then, through the crackle and airy roar of the fire, the creature let out a desperate cry. Adam watched the door cave towards him, splitting down the middle and splintering into the hallway. The fire quickly ate up the small shards of wood, sending small swirls of smoke into the air.

With the fire on the door gone, Adam saw the beast through the hazy ripple of the orange flames. She tried to take a step into the hallway, but the fire hissed on her skin, sending her back into the bedroom.

The only way out was through the window.

The window!

Adam dashed into his room, scanning it quickly. *Moby Dick* sat open on his bed. He grabbed it and his brother's baseball glove and ball and went down the steps and into the back yard again. When he got to the oak tree, he turned and looked up at the window to his mom's/beast's bedroom.

She stood in the window and Adam swore she was trying to open the window with her grimy hands. He saw the light of the fire behind her, threatening to devour the room. She turned around and then started pounding the glass. The glass would give easier than the door.

You should have taken a chance and threw some gas on her, his mind told him.

Too late to worry about that now.

Through the kitchen window, he watched the fire destroy the stairway and work on the first floor. He hugged *Moby Dick*.

He heard the grating sound of glass starting to crack. The window slowly grew multiple lines as the beast punched the window. Four jabs later, the entire window came undone. Tiny slivers of glass tinkled to the ground like snowflakes. The beast crawled through the window, the tips of the fire almost upon her.

The creature gave a powerful leap and found herself a few feet from the house. To Adam it almost appeared as if she could just start flapping her arms and fly. Except gravity took over at the end of Adam's thought and the monster began falling.

When she hit the ground, she breathed a huge grunt. Bones snapped in quite a few places and for a second she looked dead. From her deformed nose, extremely dark red blood—on the verge of being black—flowed out.

Adam waited a moment and only did that to make sure she was dead. He wasn't entirely positive the fall had killed her and if it didn't, he wanted to finish the job. He thought of the number of tools he could use.

She stirred.

Adam sprinted to the shed and grabbed the first thing on the wall nearest the door. When he was back outside, he saw it was an axe. He smiled.

The beast had crawled a few feet and when she looked up at the approaching Adam, her eyes perked up. She slowly reached out for his leg and Adam effortlessly stepped to the side. He readied the axe, aiming the sharp edge on the neck.

With the axe raised high above his head, he squeezed the handle for more power and lowered it as hard as he could.

The axe hit perfectly on the back of the creature's neck. But it didn't sever the head. It only cut about an inch deep. She bucked, but emitted no sound of pain. He lifted the axe again and brought it down harder. Or so he thought.

Her neck was like the trunk of a tree: hard and difficult to cut. The axe cut only another inch or so and still, she gave no indication there was pain. She took her hand and reached up to grab one of Adam's hands on the axe. He released with his free hand and tried to shake his captured hand to get it free.

Nothing.

The beast rose up with surprising speed and bit the axe handle and Adam's hand in the same motion. Adam screamed; intense pain wracked his arm. He fell back holding his hand, seeing his pinkie and adjacent finger gone. Blood spurted into the air.

The creature, regaining some of its strength, stretched out the limbs that Adam thought had been broken in the fall and ambled towards him.

This is it, he thought. *I tried.*

The pain in his fingers continued to send pulses to his brain, causing his eyes to flutter. *Just go away. All of it.*

Three powerful gunshots erupted in the night as Adam's eyes closed. The beast convulsed backwards, slamming into the side of the house. At that moment, the walls bowed in from the weakness the fire caused and the creature tumbled inside, flames licking her body and melting every part of her skin. He heard her screams for some odd seconds after her entry into the house. But they soon died away, haunting Adam.

Adam fainted.

CHAPTER TWENTY-TWO

Ten minutes later

Adam woke with some of the pain in his hand and arm diminished. He saw he was under the oak tree and saw the flames from the fire taking care of the rest of the house. The light from the fire cast a shadow over his face.

"You awake?" The voice came. Male, adult.

Adam nodded.

"It's Sheriff Harrington. Do you remember me?"

"Y-yes." His voice feeble.

"Good. You seem to be okay." The Sheriff looked down at Adam's hand. "Except for that."

Adam raised his arm and saw the two fingers missing and a belt wrapped around his palm, snaking to his wrist and tied tautly on his forearm. The blood still came, but a lot less now that it was somewhat secured.

"I've got an ambulance coming," he said. "Be here in about five minutes."

"Thanks."

Adam looked over and saw his bike against the tree. At least it was safe; no appendages missing from it. He laughed and then wondered one thing. "How did you know?" He asked the Sheriff.

"I got a call."

"From who?"

"You don't know?"

Adam shook his head.

"From Tommy."

"I told him not to," Adam mumbled.

The Sheriff laughed. "Well, isn't it a good thing your little brother didn't listen to you?" He got serious. "What happened here?"

Adam rolled to the side. "Camera in my pocket."

The Sheriff reached in and pulled out the digital camera.

"Pictures," Adam said.

The Sheriff turned on the camera and started flipping through the pictures. "Is this Violet's camera?"

Adam nodded, smiling. "She knows. I borrowed it from her. Keep going."

The sheriff did. Adam could tell when he reached the pictures starting with his dad. His eyebrows lowered and his mouth turned into a frown. Adam couldn't remember exactly how many pictures he'd taken, but from the look on the Sheriff's face, it seemed he took the right amount of pictures.

"I see," the Sheriff said. "When was this?"

"Last night?" Adam paused. "Or was it this morning?"

"Recent enough." The Sheriff clicked through a few more pictures. "You should have called me earlier than the other day."

"I know." Adam definitely knew that. If he would have then Tommy would probably be alive by now.

"Your brother. Did he escape?" Sheriff Harrington asked.

A few tears from Adam let the Sheriff know the answer to that question was not a positive one. The Sheriff placed a comforting hand on Adam's shoulder. "I'm sorry, he said.

Through those tears, Adam said, "Thanks. I'm glad you showed up when you did. I owe my brother my life."

"I'm sure he knows," the Sheriff said. "Your brother is proud of you, I'm sure."

"I couldn't save him."

"No, but you destroyed what destroyed him."

Was that good enough? Adam asked himself. If anything he was like Ishmael with one difference: he survived his short-lived revenge streak. Adam guessed the best thing he could do was remember Tommy forever.

In the distance, sirens wailed.

"They're coming," the sheriff said. "Everything will be okay. Just relax."

And with those six words from the reassuring voice, Adam took a deep breath and released it, letting the whole night's terrible events slide into oblivion.

EPILOGUE

Two months later.

Adam took a while to get used to his two missing fingers. He realized over the course of two months that missing his thumb would have been worse; he didn't realize most of the work of each hand involved his thumbs. Maybe he just became more conscious of that fact. The missing fingers, however, were memories of that night and would remind him each time he instinctively needed his pinkie or ring finger.

Sheriff Harrington, who requested one month later that Adam call him dad, filed paperwork to adopt Adam. The Sheriff was allowed to watch over Adam as the paperwork got approved and with the Sheriff's contacts in the county court system, it was sure to go through. Adam remained optimistic.

The house burnt completely to the ground, leaving nothing recognizable inside. Whether that was due to the fire or something else was only a guess for Adam. He saved the only things that mattered: the book, the glove and ball. The Sheriff had saved the bike at some point the following day, after everything. He asked Adam if he could get him a new bike, but Adam declined.

Adam did ask for a small area in the foyer of the Sheriff's house and a display case. The day after the request, the Sheriff bought a glass case two feet long and two feet high and mounted it on the wall in the foyer.

In the case, Adam placed the baseball glove, Tommy's favorite ball and the trophy Tommy's little league team posthumously gave to him. The plaque on the bottom of the trophy read "*Most Improved Player: Tommy*".

He could see that plaque every time he entered the house and remember Tommy forever.

ABOUT THE AUTHOR

Gregory M. Thompson is a science fiction, fantasy and horror author with credits in *Macabre Realms, Digizine, Aphelion Webzine, Concisely, Digital Dragon Magazine, Dark Gothic Resurrected* and *The Fringe Magazine.* He also has an award-nominated science fiction story in the collection, *Steampunk Anthology*, published by Sonar4 Publications.

Visit his website at www.nightcrynovel.com.

Made in the USA
Middletown, DE
12 August 2022